# ITALIAN KING

## DIRTY: A DARK MAFIA ROMANCE (MICHELI MAFIA) BOOK 1

## ZOE BETH GELLER

KINKY INK PUBLISHING

Italian King
A Dark Mafia Romance
Dirty: Dark Mafia Romance Series
(Micheli Mafia) Book 1

You can also follow me on Facebook and Amazon.

Please visit my website at zoegellerauthor.com

# CONTENTS

*To readers who enjoy a mafia book with suspense and thrills. Each book grows darker as the mystery unfolds.*

# PLAYLIST

Playlist for Dante and Juliet

*This Feeling*, The Chainsmokers
*Paris*, The Chainsmokers
*Alive*, Sia
*Last Day Alive*, The Chainsmokers, Florida Georgia Line
*Honest*, The Chainsmokers
*Wanted*, OneRepublic
*Beautiful*, Michele Marrone

# GLOSSARY

*Basta* - that's enough
   *Buon Compleanno* - Happy Birthday
   *Buongiorno* – good morning
   *Capisci* - you understand
   *Capisco* - I understand
   *Ciao* - hello, bye-bye
   *Ciao, come sta?* - Hello, how are you?
   *Chiuso* - closed
   *Cretino* - idiot, stupid
   *D'enotti* - of unknown origin (parentage)
   *Due espresso, per favore* - two espresso, please
   *Familigia* - family
   *Gelato* - ice cream with higher fat content
   *Mangia* - eat
   *Nessun problema* - no problems
   *Niente* - nothing
   *Normalmente* - normally
   *Perfetto* - perfect
   *Piazza* - square, place

GLOSSARY

*Polizia* - police
*Pronto* - ready (used to answer the telephone)
*Salute* - health
*Sì* – yes
*Va bene* - all right, okay

# CHAPTER 1

## DANTE

*I*f only the Ancient Romans could see Florence now, I muse while walking down the uneven cobblestone streets in my brown Ferragamo loafers. I take pride in the fact that my ancestors built these roads, and I'm not ashamed that I've spilled blood on them in my family's quest to carry on the family business.

Ducking inside a café, I can't keep my mouth from watering as fresh bread is pulled out of the oven and set on cooling racks. I observe commuters standing at circular high tops with no chairs. I order a cappuccino al cacao and watch the attractive fair-skinned woman in her mid-thirties steam milk until it froths. She's my type, dark hair, dark eyes. Italian with a capital I.

It's harder to find an Italian woman to date. I'm getting older, and getting married isn't my end game. And with good reason. My job is notoriously dangerous. I'd hate to inflict that upon anyone unknowingly. Nor do I wish to have children even though the birth rate of Italians has been in decline for decades. Admittedly, I have no plans to pull those statistics up.

This barista is cute and probably has a husband, based on my profiling capabilities, so I check her ring finger. Bingo. She's wearing a thin gold band, and her fingernails are worn down to the quick from hours of serving customers' coffees made to order and washing tiny plates and cups with little conversation. Our transactions are as mundane as taking a piss every morning.

No flashy engagement ring—that's not the European way. Unless you are incredibly wealthy, that is. And I am. However, would I ever buy an engagement ring? I scoff at the mere thought of it. My family knows I'm never getting married, as much as my mother may hound me. I'm committed to my plans.

I might be the most sought-after bachelor in the city, but I don't need to be married to have wicked sex with any woman I desire. I thrive on my freedom and feel no obligations past a hookup. Women tell me what they think I want to hear, hoping to please me or appease me; I'm not sure. Nothing will change the fact that I will only give them as much as I want—a night filled with sex as hot as our summer sun and little conversation. I am a poser when I wear my dignified routine in businessman suits tailored for powerful meetings with legitimately powerful people. I'm in my prime with money to burn, and that causes women to swoon at my feet.

Like bees to nectar, it's too easy, and it bores me. My only obligation is to my family, the interests I have to protect, and the things I need to do to ensure our survival in a ruthless, dark world. One that sharply contrasts the normalcy afforded most individuals who know what to expect every day of their life.

This train station is always busy, so it's a perfect spot for me to blend in and remain invisible, and for the most part, it works. Only my enemies and my trail of broken-hearted ex-girlfriends would spot me in public. To everyone else, I'm a face without a name, and I like to keep it that way. It's safer for me. It's safer for everyone.

To avoid danger, I stay on the move, avoiding repetitive patterns in my daily routine. I learned this strategy early from my grandfather, Diego Micheli. These days, he lives on a tiny island off the coast of Tuscany, where he enjoys beautiful sunsets over the

Tyrrhenian Sea, but at one time, he was the most powerful don in Italy.

I rarely have time to visit him anymore, as I'm too busy to take time away from work, and I know he understands. After all, if my dad hadn't died so young, I wouldn't have been called upon to head the family businesses.

I'm also too busy for love. Love is strictly off-limits, a luxury I can't afford. It's a blessing and a curse, but that's what it means to be at the head of the table.

I take my eyes off the female barista long enough to check out the sandwiches in the case. The ham and cheese panini looks particularly good. So does the caprese.

There is a clink as the ceramic saucer is set on the marble counter. The white froth is in the shape of a heart and is dusted with cocoa. Perfetto. I use the sugar crystals on a stick resting on the saucer, and I slowly stir the hot brew, giving it a minute to cool. For a moment, I can relax and not think about work.

When she asks if I'd like anything else, I order a chocolate-filled cornetto. This café gets its pastries handmade by local bakers, and I've always been partial to them. They aren't overly sweet, but that doesn't prevent them from being irresistible.

The woman brings me the dessert wrapped in wax paper to go. I finish it in two bites before downing my cappuccino in one gulp. I pay the cashier and exit, stepping onto the cracked sidewalk.

The temperature is still cool and will increase as the sun rises. I stroll back to my Mercedes SUV and ignore the judgmental stares from the elderly men sitting at the outdoor neighborhood café. No doubt they think I'm greedy for having a gas-guzzling vehicle. My tires have been slashed for that in the past. I smile and say, "Buongiorno," as I pass them. They remain silent.

Ordinarily, I'm a man of few words, and my work face is stoic. I haven't met a woman yet who can make me change my ways. I only let my family see the human side of me, the one that is capable of a chuckle if the situation warrants it. Mama worries about me, but she worries about everything incessantly. That's an Italian mother for you.

Cars speed past, and horns honk as I approach the city, which is bustling with early morning activity. I have an important meeting with my contact and my bodyguard, and my right-hand man, Riccardo. Normally, he is with me, but I like to keep life simple and enjoy a few minutes in the morning to be myself and not the monster I've become to keep things going after Dad died. In most places, he'd be called Papa. In Tuscany we say Babbo.

My father's heart attack two years ago was a blow to my family. I had hoped it might spell the end of the long-standing feud with the Conti family in the South, but it was not to be. Papa always said, "Once an enemy, always an enemy," and with good reason—he was younger than me when he lost his brother in a turf war with the Contis. In fact, both families lost a son before the killing spilled into the streets.

I want to think we are more civilized than other countries. Today, I'm not so sure. The Sicilians have contacts in most continents; I'm content with Italy and use other resources on an as-needed basis.

I make my way down to the non-touristy area of the magnificent city, driving past warehouses owned by Chinese, Russian, and Albanian companies. I am far from my mansion in Fiesole, where the view overlooking the city of Florence is astounding. To get to Fiesole, one has to ascend a long and winding road. This provides a good vantage point over possible intruders, which was a selling point for me.

I maneuver down the crowded streets until I arrive at a café and park on the street. Riccardo is waiting for me, standing by the door, dressed in a black dress shirt and pants.

I stroll toward him and say, "Good morning." He nods.

We sit on wooden chairs around a small metal table overlooking a neighborhood park near the Arno River.

"Well?" I ask.

"I think we found her. We're just waiting on Michael."

I nod. Without asking, an espresso is placed on the table—they know me. I pour a packet of sugar into the strong brew before taking a sip. Ah, I can never have too many in a day.

Michael arrives dressed in a tracksuit and pulls up a chair. He's a trusted associate, a hired man to do whatever we need. He's a decent man who accepts the fact his job description is always subject to change.

"Michael." I nod, acknowledging him and finishing my drink in one gulp. "What's the word?"

"I found her. She's in college here in Florence, studying art," he replies. His dark brown hair is full and slicked back, but his receding hairline makes him look older than his mid-twenties.

"Are you sure it's her?"

"I did all the research, just like you asked. No one knows anything, which is why it took some time. I'm the only one who handled it, so there's no trail to her—or you." He emphasizes the last word heavily.

I run my hand across my mouth and clean-shaven jaw, which I habitually do when I'm deep in thought. I nod again as I play with the tiny spoon on the saucer.

"You're fucking kidding me." Riccardo lets out a low whistle. "Conti is going to shit his pants. His best-kept secret, the jewel of his empire. Has she really been discovered?"

"Keep your eye on her, get to know her routine, but don't let her see you."

"Done." Michael stands. Riccardo follows suit and slips him an envelope of cash.

"Mr. Micheli." Michael nods to me and disappears. He knows I'm a man who prefers results over extended chatter.

"So, what's your plan?" Riccardo sits down again. He's fit for a man in his mid-forties. His salt-and-pepper beard is impeccably trimmed, and his clothing is always a notch above casual wear. Like all Italians, he likes his designers.

"First, I'll put out a feeler for a meet with Giovanni Conti. Then we'll go from there. Not a word to anyone." I don't really have to remind him, yet I say it anyway. "We have no idea what his reaction will be, and we must tread carefully."

I have to push the issue with Conti to get what's ours. However, there is a fine line between pushing and making him think I don't respect him. And since he is a known psychopath, I hate having to deal with him at all.

I have good men like Riccardo around me. I picked him because he knew what to do without me telling him, and he worked his way up the ranks. He follows through without flinching at any task, big or small. He also has a military background which can't hurt.

I see him checking out people walking by, and if I asked him what car just passed us, he would give me the correct answer. The man's memory, like his loyalty, is never in question, and he always has my back. I demand loyalty above all else because, in the mafia, it comes down to loyalty and trust to stay alive.

# CHAPTER 2

## JULIET

*I*f only my dad liked to travel. But he doesn't, so I'm stuck in Tuscany. 'Stuck' is the wrong word for it. It's beautiful, but there are so many places in this beautiful country to explore. Pranzano, Rome, and Siena are just a few I'd love to see. I'll get there someday.

"You look like a princess!" my roommate, Ava, gushes as she puts a fake tiara on my head like I'm a ten-year-old. When do girls get over this princess shit, anyway? I don't see it. She's from the United States and came all this way just for a summer internship in Florence. Now, that's what I call a princess lifestyle. If one goes anywhere to study art, this is the place for it. Home of the Greats, I like to call it.

Don't get me wrong, I like Ava, but she's only here for the summer. She's from New York, Long Island, to be exact. She says it a bit funny, overpronouncing the last vowels and dragging them out.

She giggles. "Well, in New York, all the girls from wealthy Italian and Jewish families are princesses. Then you have the CAP, the Catholic American Princesses, and the JAP, the Jewish American Princesses. The tiara has become a staple for all teenage girls on their birthdays."

She snags the tiara off my head and plops it atop her long, blond locks. "We are getting a bit old for it, though, aren't we?" Her nose crinkles as she speaks, and her voice fades out.

"I'll say," I agree, never having fantasized about being a princess. I'm an ordinary girl in an ordinary world. I never imagine any man is checking me out because they are always looking at other girls, the ones who can curl eyelashes without poking their eyes out. The girls who know how to put together a flawless outfit. Girls like Ava.

Did my father adore me? Yes, of course, and I'm grateful for it. It probably kept me from hanging out with bad boys and pursuing the wrong kind of attention out of loneliness.

"So, what do you want to do today? Being Saturday and all, we have the whole weekend ahead of us." She flits excitedly around the room, using her phone to turn up the music streaming from a portable speaker she lugged thousands of miles to use for two months.

"Whatever you like," I reply. I don't have any plans. I live a quiet life compared to most girls my age. I'm more comfortable being alone than I am with a crowd of acquaintances. Maybe it's because I'm an only child and the town I grew up in is so small it wouldn't even be on a map were it not for the handmade pottery the tourists stop to admire.

Ava's company is a welcome change from the girls who are more into their boyfriends than their studies. She is a foreigner who came to paint our jaw-dropping scenery, eat our amazing food, and join me in the dorm to live like a local Florentine for the summer.

I'm happy to have her as a friend. The campus thins out in the summertime, and the number of tourists escalates to the point it's hard to walk anywhere. The sidewalks are always packed.

I like hearing about America and hope to visit someday, but for now, I'm content to live here. This is my home. I can't imagine living anywhere else. But someday? Put me on a plane, and I'll go anywhere.

"Maybe we can find a pretty spot and work on a sketch and then practice with oils on it later," I venture enthusiastically.

"That sounds like fun. It's gorgeous outside. Afterward, we can grab a sandwich at our favorite place and have a glass of wine."

"Ava, it's ten o'clock in the morning!"

"Oh, don't roll your eyes at me. You know you love a great Sangiovese," she teases me.

I can't deny it.

"Okay, let me just pack some art supplies." I open a cloth tote and put in my 11 x 14 sketchbook and my boxes of treasured charcoals.

I glance over at Ava, who's fluffing up her hair and painting her smile a little thicker than I would, using bright red lipstick.

"I'm just going to add some bronzer to my face. Then we can head out," I announce, so she knows to be ready. Looking like a model takes time, is one lesson I've learned from her. Not that I aspire to be a model, but I wouldn't turn down an offer of help if it makes me appear more accomplished. I never feel like I fit in.

Ava is the first roommate I've had who doesn't have a steady boyfriend. I don't have one either, never have. My take on boyfriends is that they consume and monopolize a girl's entire life. Girls drop everything when a man comes along. I mean, is it the guy? The thrill of something new? Or is the sex so great that women forget all their dreams and goals when they drop out of school? That's happened to more than one of my classmates.

Even though I'm young and have this incredible, vibrant city at my disposal, I find it hard to connect with the other students. I'm not one for joining clubs. Making new friends is intimidating for me. I never get an invite to hang out with other students or attend off-campus parties. I have no one to blame but myself. These are hurdles I envisioned I'd have leaped over by this point. At twenty-one, the expectation was to have made more headway toward my career ambitions. Mom dubs me a 'late bloomer.' Perhaps she's right.

At the end of summer, I'll get another roommate. I don't like not knowing who I'll get in the roommate lotto, but Dad thinks it's safer for me to live in the dorms. I'm sure he knows best. Rent in the city is crazy expensive. I don't want my parents going broke paying for me to pursue my dreams, dreams that may never materialize. It's difficult to break into the art scene anywhere, let alone here! But I want to work in the creative field as that's my true calling. I can't shut down my creative thoughts, whether it is colors in a painting, dreaming up furniture designs, or settling into graphic artwork. I'm savvy with all the software artists use.

"Ready," Ava announces as she walks to the door with her tote in hand, one matching mine. They were given to us at summer registration and have our school's emblem on them with the fleur-de-lis. I lock the door behind us before we enter the courtyard, where students gather on benches. They draw the surrounding evergreens lining the banks of the Arno River. The trees provide welcome shade as well as a touch of nature to the heart of the city.

I'm wearing a cherry red sundress as it's warm outside. The color complements my olive skin. My skin is darker than most Tuscans and definitely darker than my parents. We joke that someone in the family tree must have married a Sicilian.

The courtyard has students coming and going, and I hear shouts and car horns honking on busy streets. The noise bounces off the surrounding buildings.

"It's the dean," Ava nudges my arm with her elbow.

"Really?"

"Oh, yes, he's involved in the exchange program. Like a goodwill ambassador, I guess. And look at that hunk talking to him!"

I check out the man standing next to Dean Santini. The stranger is dressed in black, and even though it's just a casual dress shirt and slacks with leather shoes, he looks sharp, like James Bond without the jacket and tie. He preens like a peacock, proud and confident. The dean appears to shrink in his shadow.

"I wonder who he is."

"No idea. I've never seen him before, but boy, I wish I had," she murmurs quietly as we draw closer to him.

Ava puts one hand casually on her Marc Jacobs tote and slides her canvas bag onto the same arm, leaving one hand free as we approach.

I shy away, but they are standing near our exit, making it difficult for me not to engage should the situation arise.

"Good morning, ladies," the dean addresses Ava with a smile, so we stop and chat.

It's such an Italian thing to do, to take time out for a brief chat with an acquaintance or a friend when you casually bump into them. There is never an excuse that you're in a hurry because in Italy, everything can be a few minutes late and it's never a problem.

"Hello, how are you?"

"Just fine, thank you. I want to introduce you to Mr. Micheli. He's one of our benefactors here at the school."

"I love the arts," Mr. Micheli adds without a smile.

Ava extends her hand to the sexy stranger, who takes it in his before leaning in to exchange the traditional small kiss on both cheeks before turning to me.

"Nice to meet you . . ." He leaves the sentence unfinished, suspended in the air between us.

"Juliet. Juliet Accordi." I gaze up at him through my long lashes, captivated by his intense brown eyes holding my gaze. "It's nice to meet you." I notice his face is cold and his voice devoid of emotion.

"Likewise," he says as he leans in to kiss my right cheek, then my left. The hair on the back of my neck stands up at his touch. "Are you enjoying your studies here?"

"Oh, yes," I assure him. My flesh tingles with mixed feelings, excited on the one hand and scared on the other. I have no idea what is triggering this fight-or-flight response. I want to follow my body's urge to run and leave immediately, but I don't want it to look obvious.

He turns his attention back to Ava and chats with her for a minute, but I can't help feeling he's watching me even though his eyes are clearly on her.

There is something about him, but I can't put my finger on it. He's observant and a man of few words, which implies he's either very smart or he's used to playing things close to his chest.

He's definitely sure of himself, his posture exuding strength and virility. I bet he has us both committed to memory, and he probably has me pegged right down to my black bikini underwear.

"Would you ladies like to join us for an espresso?" he asks, looking at both of us as the church bells from the Duomo chime and echo down the city streets.

We wait for the bells to finish before resuming our conversation.

"Thank you, but we were just heading out," I explain, putting my arm firmly through Ava's.

"Another time then, perhaps," he says, wishing us a good afternoon before he nods and walks away with the dean in the opposite direction.

After we exit the courtyard, I turn my head to take one more look at the handsome stranger when I overhear him asking the dean about the art program and the future funding needed, but I can't catch any details after that.

"That was weird." I still have my arm through Ava's as we hit the narrow sidewalk, making our way to our favorite park near the river. The sky is partially cloudy, so the water will not look blue today, which is a pity. I'll have to tweak the color later. I hate the look of muddy water.

"What? He seemed perfectly fine," she replies as we step inside the café on the corner for a quick espresso.

"Due espresso, per favore," I pull euros out of my knock-off Gucci purse I wear slung from my shoulders and across my chest to prevent it from being ripped off by a professional pickpocket. The city is rife with them.

I had to teach Ava how to do these things, or she would have lost her expensive camera on her first day of sightseeing.

I pay the man behind the counter for our drinks and buy bottled water as well. I can feel the day heating up as moisture builds on the nape of my neck.

"Do I look flushed?" I stir a packet of sugar into my espresso and turn to face her.

"God, I'm addicted to this." Ava lets her drink cool for thirty seconds before downing it in two gulps before she checks out my face. "Nope, you're fine. Maybe it was that hot Italian dude making you sweat," she snickers.

"Well . . ." I fumble for words as I remember the chance meeting.

"Well, what? Hottie! He had an air of mystery or danger about him," she volunteers. "You have everything here in Italy—hot men, coffee, food, tons of antiquities to take in. It's amazing. I love it."

"We're pretty lucky." Grateful for the distraction of the mystery man, we stroll down to the park and find a free bench. We need an entire bench to ourselves as our art supplies fill up all the empty space between us.

Birds chirp in the lush trees overhead as Ava asks me how to say 'Happy birthday' in Italian. She tries to say, 'Buon compleanno,' but botches it terribly, and we both laugh at her attempts.

I appreciate that she's trying to learn, but honestly, foreigners can get around easily without knowing any Italian, at least in the city. Most waiters will know English so they can earn better tips. Many of the under thirty-year-olds speak English because it was integrated into our schools three decades ago.

But it helps to know some Italian to get around outside of the large tourist areas. Granted, the train stations sell tickets from kiosk machines with English signage. Tickets for the city buses are sold in small shops where one can buy items like newspapers, candy, cigars, and cheap souvenirs, and you need Italian to get by in those as the worker is probably from another country and only knows two languages. So, I continue to teach her a little of the language as we go.

# CHAPTER 3

## DANTE

*R*iccardo remains on the street, inconspicuously leaning against the stone building while I walk under the Roman arches and inside to my appointment with the dean.

I find him sitting in his office behind an antique desk that's probably older than he is. Standing as I walk in, we shake hands, and he offers me a tour of the immediate campus.

Funny how a busy dean is suddenly available when the word 'donation' is dropped into his lap like a fresh-baked cookie. I keep my conversation light and superficial as if I'm here on a whim.

There's no reason why I can't become a patron of the arts. Most people in my circle assume 'the arts' are opera, ballet, or theater, but I'm of the opinion art is art, and what's wrong with helping a school that might inspire a sculptor or painter who goes on to become famous? Or, at the very least, make a living doing what they love? For an artist, it's tough.

The dean is not a particularly distinguished man in his early sixties, about the same age my dad would be had he survived his heart attack. Does he know I'm a member of the Micheli family, as in the Family? I don't know, but I follow him around and listen with polite interest, and for his time, he'll get a generous donation.

When he asks what I do, I say I'm the CEO of Micheli Enterprises, and our main focus is construction. It's a long-running joke in my family after the tiny bathroom in Mama's condo cost a fortune and took forever. Let's just say, you never, ever pay for a job upfront.

I'm not totally lying when I say we're in construction. We do have our hand in that, but we're also into guns. By this, I mean our crews run the streets and the drugs. I can't be picky because anything I don't deal with, my competition will. With the euro coming in and the economy hitting the skids, I now have to worry about money and power-hungry factions who encroach on our territory and sales.

The factions I have to watch today are amateurs from other countries and aren't as organized as we are. They are just happy to take any opportunity they see if it means they can pocket a few euros.

Let's face facts, I have a huge list of officials, polizia, and others on my payroll. Everyone can be bought or leveraged. Human trafficking is huge, too, although I have a distaste for it myself and forbid my capos from 'hopping on that bandwagon,' as they say in America.

Back in the day, it would have been the political party factions, terrorists from other countries, and rogue military upstarts looking for high-grade explosives and tons of guns. Since then, the list has evolved, and with today's open borders, gun sales are never going to go down. Hell, one of our country's largest export sectors is domestically made weapons.

Even if the dean knew I was the head of the family, one associated with the mafia, he'd be a fool not to take my money. Everyone knows if you treat your mafia friends well, and don't act stupid, we're harmless.

Today was just an impromptu visit and by sheer luck I stumbled into my mark at the end of the tour. I can't believe how fortuitous this is, but then again, I'm a very lucky man. Things just fall into place for me at the damnedest times, and I never question it for fear I might jinx it.

I wouldn't have minded coffee with the girls, but they declined, so I'm done here. I skillfully evade the dean's invitation for lunch. As I leave the courtyard, I glance both ways, checking my surroundings. It's instinct and survival.

"So?" Riccardo questions me with one word as we make our way to my black Range Rover.

"I actually met her as she was leaving. She, and another girl who was with her, Ava, was her name."

"Must be a friend," Riccardo says as he slips behind the wheel.

"Maybe. Ava's not Italian, I can tell you that. She dresses like big city, American." My brows furrow. "When do we meet with Conti?"

I'm anxious to get my plan underway, one way or another. If I need to use the backup plan, well, after meeting Juliet, I'm not opposed to having her to myself for a week.

"I'll have everything confirmed today. It's tricky, getting so close to the enemy's territory."

"It's going to be at a trattoria near the Colosseum among a million tourists in broad daylight."

"True."

"More blood's been spilled for less," Riccardo reminds me.

I shrug my shoulders and look out the window as we head to lunch.

While I go inside the restaurant, Riccardo stays outside to talk on his phone and smoke a vape pen, having given up cigarettes yet again. I can always tell the first few days as he's cranky and irritated at every little thing. Hopefully, the vape isn't as bad for him.

I order in his absence. I can't resist the charcuterie board and order one for us to share. The fresh meat and cheese are just what I need to get through the rest of the day, and it's a special treat to drizzle honey on the creamy burrata. I never bother at home. It's plenty of food for both of us, and I order two glasses of red wine to go with it.

Riccardo sits, and he receives the text he's been waiting on.

"Tomorrow. We'll take the jet to Rome. It's all set." For a man who's normally not nervous, he seems on edge.

"What's up?"

"I'll be glad when it's over," he admits. "We'll take three more guards with us."

I nod. I trust him with my life, and he's the expert. I take a bite of the bruschetta, and Riccardo dives into the meat.

He knows better than to ask what my plan is, trusting me to fill him in when appropriate. We've known each other for years, and it's the way we've always worked together.

"I'm more concerned about the girl. That will be... laborious." His grin falls short of a smile. "She is beautiful. Can't believe that ugly Conti produced her. She must take after her mother."

"Probably." I chuckle and take a sip of my red wine, letting it slide down my throat. I'm not in a rush.

"So, Rome tomorrow. I'm not looking forward to rubbing elbows with the tourists on the streets. No doubt the city will be packed."

"We'll buffer for you, boss. It's a quick meet, in and out," he reassures me as he drinks from his wine glass.

I ask him to put the University on our list of organizations we'll support and stress that a check won't be going out quite yet. I'm the only one with the playbook in my head on how to make sure Conti gives us what we need. But the dean will see his money eventually. It's the least I can do for a preview of Juliet.

Besides, a check showing up at the university at the wrong time would not be beneficial to me, or to Conti. Today, we're just getting the lay of the land, should we have to resort to our backup plan. I'm not normally one to kidnap women, but drastic times call for drastic measures if need be.

"Once we have the Port of Civitavecchia agreement enforced, we'll be able to ramp up the quotas on everything. This is huge." I almost smile. This is my life, my entire life. I live to work, and I work to live. I also love a great Italian red wine and a good fucking lay whenever the mood hits.

Riccardo tosses his head back as he drops another piece of prosciutto into his mouth and lets out a hearty chuckle.

"What?"

"You almost broke a smile," he accuses me of something he knows I rarely do.

"Hmm, maybe," I acknowledge. What he doesn't know is, as much as I'm excited about brokering an easy deal with the Conti family, I'm still thinking about the vixen at the school.

Juliet totally oozed sex appeal without even trying. She had no idea the way the low-cut sundress was showing off her firm breasts and sun-kissed shoulders, or how the light breeze was lifting the hem of her dress and teasing me with peeks at her long legs, toned from walking or possibly the gym. She couldn't have walked far from campus today, not wearing those wedge heels.

Her whole vibe came across as classy, mature, but shy. The only makeup she wore was lipstick, and with her natural beauty, it's all she needed. It makes my cock eager for some pussy as I sit here remembering every detail. I find her sexier than fuck, and one way or another, I will have her. I always get what I want.

We finish lunch with an espresso before making our way to the accountant. He's more of a money launderer than an accountant. He tells me everything is in order and I'm relieved no one is dipping their hand into my pocket, so the home front is happy. I have to be accountable to my family.

After leaving the accountant, Riccardo drives us along Via dei Calzaiuoli where all the upscale shops are located, where the women love to shop for designer purses, shoes, and anything else they can buy with their wealthy old husbands' money.

Today is no different. Women buzz in and out of shops while their husbands sit at outdoor cafés sipping thick Italian wine and enjoying the ambiance of the city streets with the sounds of ambulance sirens and bells of the *duomo* in the background.

It starts raining as we arrive at our meeting with a boss who helps to wash money in his laundromat because it's so easy to throw in more cash. It's important to show up so they know I'm around, and it's an incentive to keep work matters above board.

Afterward, we head back to the Range Rover so I can drive my Mercedes home. It would be nice to get home at a reasonable time for a change and use my expensive swimming pool, but the rain makes traffic come to a standstill.

The rain lets up. Riccardo is still following me as we snake our way up the hill to Viale Augusto Righi and into the Piazza Mino da Fiesole. We don't have any more pressing business left for today. I'll be home in time to enjoy a dip in the pool as the rain has stopped, and I have time before dinner.

I glance over at my favorite place to eat on the corner of the piazza before proceeding up another hill to where my mansion awaits. It's a winding road, and it can be treacherous in winter if there is ice on the road.

Riccardo pulls up beside me at the large Tuscan estate and walks ahead of me to open my front door. He clears the house as I head to the kitchen pulling a chilled Moretti Beer out of the refrigerator. The night guards are already on the property, and once Riccardo is satisfied the house is secure, and the video feeds are working as they should, he leaves for the night.

Alone in the house, my mind drifts back to Juliet, her delicate eyes haunting me. Her unassuming innocence and lightness were in stark contrast to the darkness of her hair, so dark it shone. If it were a moonless night, I'd never find her. I can tell by her dark olive complexion she's not a typical Tuscan. Is it possible she knows she's not who she thinks she is?

Why do I care one way or the other, anyway?

I don't relish meeting my grandfather's and father's nemesis tomorrow, but the meeting has to take place as I have big plans, and he's the lynchpin. I need the port he controls to fulfill our projections made two years ago, projections we made with control of the port factored in.

I pull my phone out of my pocket and step onto my patio overlooking an infinity pool costing more than most homes down the hill in Florence. I see my maid has put pillows on the lounge chair in anticipation of my arrival, and I decide to sit and kick my shoes off and enjoy the late afternoon.

Beer in one hand, phone in the other, I decide to text Alessia. She's a sure thing who won't mind if I'm calling her for a night of pleasure.

She texts me back right away as if she's been waiting all day for me to get in touch with her. It must be a tough life blowing your monthly allowance and waiting for texts from a random guy. I'd be impressed with a woman who has aspirations of what she wants to become in life rather than one who is waiting around for a marriage proposal.

We met years ago at a club, and while I don't go clubbing as much as I used to, she's one fling who continues to come and go over the years. Maybe she's waiting for me to change my mind, I don't know. Not my problem.

My best chance to avoid emotional involvement is not keeping a woman around for too long. I can't share the details of my life with anyone. I don't allow anyone to get close to me. It's the best way to keep the organization off the radar. Even if someone gets caught, they wouldn't know enough to give the police substantial evidence of any crimes.

She knows the rules. One sign she's into me too much, and she'll get her walking papers, just like the countless women who came before her.

# CHAPTER 4

## JULIE

*O*n our way back to the university, we have to deal with the summer's sea of tourists meandering everywhere. Sometimes the sidewalks are so packed that people take to the streets but it's a recipe for disaster. The only time of year we don't have to contend with crowds is December to February, when it's rainy, windy, and can be frigid as fuck.

Ava and I happen to be walking too close to the street when I hear a motorcycle coming. The driver isn't paying attention to how close he is, so I quickly yank her out of the way.

"Sheesh, Ava," I scold her, "What the hell? You almost got hit."

"Thanks, I guess I wasn't paying attention," she says, still shaking from the close encounter.

"Well, I still don't see how our drivers here are worse than what you get in New York like you said, but yeah, you need to be more careful."

"Let's stop at the little café by the university for a panini," she suggests while waiting to cross the street in front of the school making sure the cars stop before crossing over.

My stomach rumbles in agreement, and I double-check the traffic before we cross, taking her arm protectively. I notice some dark SUV-type vehicles on the street and think of the mysterious man from the courtyard. I wonder if he drives one of those. He seemed powerful, maybe even secretive as he offered nothing about himself in our friendly encounter.

We place our food order at the counter and look around for a place to sit. It's a tiny hole in the wall with limited seating so I eye the tables wondering who will leave first. We sat for over an hour drawing. The walk here helped get the blood flowing back to my legs and feet, but my feet are now sore and ready for these wedge shoes to come off. I'd much rather be home eating lunch and walking around in my bare feet.

"Oh, table," I call out and make a beeline for the two-top a couple has just vacated.

"Great!" Ava follows on my heels just as our order number is called.

"I got the table. You take care of the food."

She carries the food to our table whereby I quickly grab my fresh off-the-press panini. Eagerly taking my first bite of the gold and crisp crust, I immediately regret it. It's way too fucking hot and I open my mouth in an attempt to not burn my tongue. I should know better, but I'm so hungry, I'd kill anyone who tried to rip it out of my hands.

"You goof, you know it's hot. Those panini machines are bitching," she comments as she lifts hers to her lips and cautiously blows on it before taking a bite. "I have to tell you, your electrical appliances here are Gods, or the food is just fucking amazing." She sinks her teeth into the meat and cheese with gusto.

"It's our food, no preservatives, locally baked bread, no GMOs or whatever the hell they call them."

"I'm so going to miss this."

"Ava, you still have weeks here, don't think about it. Just enjoy."

I pop the top of my water bottle and drink to wash down the sandwich. My taste buds are loving this sandwich, and my tummy is happy to be fed.

"I can't wait to paint in my sketch. I think it came out nice."

"It did. Mine needs some work. I can't wait for the anatomy class." She gives me a naughty grin.

"Oh, I bet." I chuckle. "It's not such a big deal here, but yeah, the models are super-hot. Fine specimens."

"I bet. Like I said, can't wait!" She gives me an impish grin and turns me inside out.

We dump our trash and make the short walk to our dorm. The streets are busy, even though many local shops are closed for the few hours they take off in the afternoon. One shutter is being pulled down over the shop's frontage as we pass, and I hear the rollers make a rickety sound as the thin metal bumps and buckles roll over the tracks like they have countless times before.

The shopkeeper turns the sign to read, '*Chiuso*' and hurries away to enjoy his mid-afternoon break.

The cloudy sky suddenly turns dark, and raindrops begin to fall, taking me by surprise. I never carry an umbrella, but I can't run home in these shoes either so I'm getting soaked.

"Ahh," I yell out to no one in particular as the rain starts out with a few drops and turns into a monsoon. Ava races ahead of me.

If not for the rain, I might not have noticed the two men hanging out on the sidewalk dressed in expensive black t-shirts, heavy, not cheap, with black pants. Their arms folded across their chests, they looked like they were waiting for someone until the rain forced them to take cover under a nearby awning.

I know what they are. The movie *John Wick* isn't lost on me. Organized crime never sleeps. We don't think much about it as locals, it becomes part of the background, but we all know the elements are constantly swirling around us. It's part of the landscape living and breathing next to us every day. It's not just the tourists who fall victim to the mafia's sophisticated systems. Occasionally, we do too.

By the time we return to the dorms, my hair is dripping wet and hanging in strands around my face like mascara that ran. God knows I can't put it on to save my life, so it's a good thing I didn't wear any mascara with the cloudburst going on. I'd look like a raccoon.

My sundress is dripping on the old marble flooring that's indestructible. The cold chill is making my nipples taut in my bra and the hair on my arms stands up. Gathering up my long dark hair, I wring out the excess water and watch it puddle at my feet in the entranceway.

"Whoo." I take a breath and rub my arms.

"Come, you need a towel." Ava starts walking down the hallway toward our room. I follow knowing a hot shower will be a welcomed relief as soon as we get there.

I don't think twice about the two men in the street I saw under the awning. It's not like I would know the names or faces of any crime families in Italy. Who are they waiting for? I've had a weird vibe all day and wonder if I missed something, but nobody would be interested in me.

Ava unlocks our door, and we drop our wet bags on the floor whereby I immediately pull out my sketch pad, set it on my desk, and carefully open the damp pages so they can dry.

Shoes fly off next. "Dibs on the shower." I step out of my wet dress, leaving it on the now damp floor as I scamper to the tiny bathroom where I'll warm up under the hot water. But not before I prance on my tiptoes to warm up while I wait for the hot water to make it through the old pipes.

I'm turned on and horny as hell as I step under the warm water at last. I'm wet between my legs—and it's not from the rain. Horny and wet. I don't think twice before I slide my hand down to my engorged lips and massage myself. I have a hand on my left breast as my right one finds my nub and those familiar feelings of desire wash over me like a waterfall, all-consuming as I tune out the world.

Except for Mr. Sexy Eyes handsome face, his warm eyes and deep voice enhance my pleasure as I gasp when I come with little effort. It's been so long since I've been laid it felt good to have something stiff inside me even if it was only my fingers. The release —a needed outlet for pent-up sexual frustration from the last hookup I had didn't go anywhere.

I'm relaxed now with a warm glow as I dry my hair using a wall plug near my bed so Ava can have a turn in the bathroom. My hair is so long, and blow drying takes forever. It wouldn't take as long if I just gave in and cut it back to my shoulders, but I like it this way.

I pull on a pair of shorts with a few holes in them, shorter than Mama would approve of. I pull on a tee with the university logo and put my hair in a ponytail before settling on my creaky bed to think about my picture. Art always seems to be on my mind. When sketching, it's all about getting the light right and deciding the best angle. Is it a portrait or a photojournalist approach?

Ava is back from her shower and chatting away with her family back home, providing a rhythmic backdrop to the rain pelting the tiled roof. A clap of thunder makes her jump and rattles the tiny windows in our small room.

I stream an Italian opera channel to my earbuds and lie back on my twin bed. Placing my sketchbook on my lap, I pull colored charcoal from the box where I keep them stowed in slots to prevent them from breaking.

I draw a young couple kissing by the river and threw in some large trees for composition. Using the charcoals to fill in the white areas on my paper, I pay close attention to the colors needed to get the desired depth and reflection of the light.

I sink back into my pillows and rest my picture on my knees as I work with the powdery chalk that rubs off on my fingertips, I blend it here and there to obtain the desired effect. I smile and softly murmur the words to the song I'm listening to. I notice another bolt of lightning and thunder rumbles outside, but I'm safe, warm, and happy inside my room. I love loud storms and find them relaxing.

My phone clicks in my ear which means Mama is texting me.

She's wondering how I am and wants to visit the city to spend a day with me. She says Dad might come too, but if we're doing anything other than dinner or a movie, he'll stay home because watching women shop is torture to him. That last part makes me laugh.

I text her about my day, sending her a snapshot of my present project and letting her know I love her before she has to go make dinner for dear old Dad. I ask her to give Dad a hug for me and glance over at Ava, sitting on her bed with her legs crossed. I notice she's finished her call with her mother.

"How's your picture?"

I flip it around to show her.

"You are wicked good," she smiles, "you really have talent."

"Thanks."

The storm lets up by nightfall, and we dash to the cafeteria for pizza. By the time we finish eating, it's turned into a beautiful summer evening, so we grab a gelato around the corner for dessert.

Gone are most of the tourists this time of night. Now, it's just us and a few locals as we make our way to the gelateria. We ask for two scoops of lemon in a cup and eat it as we walk back to the dorms, and I forget about the men dressed in black.

# CHAPTER 5

## DANTER

*A*s much as it goes against my code, I can't help but wonder if I will want an heir at some point in my life. Targeting wives and children used to be considered off-limits, but today it's not. To put someone in that kind of danger is not something to be taken lightly. For my generation, having kids outside of marriage is growing in popularity, but I still think any kind of family is a responsibility and a liability. I vowed never to have a wife or child, and, seeing as how I'm the leader of our famiglia, it's been quietly accepted.

Much has changed over the years, and at times, I think maybe it is a blessing Babbo didn't survive the massive heart attack that killed him two years ago. I loved him, but I know he couldn't leave the past behind in order to keep up with changing times. Change is hard for anyone, but most men of his stature and background liked to do business with a handshake or over a glass of scotch and a smooth cigar.

I could sense his frustration with the younger generation. They tried their best to work for him, but the young kids were the bane of his existence. There was a dangerous disconnect which was frustrating for all parties concerned. Ultimately, I viewed this as a liability to the organization and leadership saw it as a managerial weakness. For most of us, our underlings are mediocre at best. Like every business, good help is hard to find.

Babbo didn't grow up with privilege and wealth. Grandpa had plenty of money but lived conservatively. Always prepared for turf wars, strikes at ports, and whatever other nonsense came under the loose term of 'doing business,' he kept the organization going as the landscape around him changed.

Lean times hit during the war with the Contis, but the worst part was it spilled onto the streets and resulted in hits on the sons of both families. After both the Contis and the Michelis lost a son to hits, both families agreed things needed to deescalate.

But it was too late. Soon, our faces were forever on the news, making our names synonymous with violence, drugs, and other despicable things like human trafficking that I, to this day, refuse to be a part of.

Babbo took over years later, and when he died, no foul play was suspected in his heart attack, but I beefed up security anyway. Once an enemy, always an enemy.

Growing up, I remember he adamantly refused to take aspirin for a headache. He never went to the doctor, preferring Grandma's homemade chicken soup over any pill.

No one knew he had heart issues, and no one could have guessed how sick he was until he dropped to the ground. But I knew Babbo and knew he would have preferred it to be quick rather than being a burden or lingering on, knowing the end was coming.

Quick deaths in our world are the norm because that's how it goes. A deal goes sideways, someone gets cocky, attitudes are out of control, and shit happens.

I finish my beer, leaving the empty bottle under the lounger, and make my way inside carrying my leather dress shoes. Alessia rang at the security gate and is now driving up in her Italian-made Spider, red of course.

I open the door to see her walking up and looking stunning in an evening dress. She's dressed to go out dancing more so than staying home to fuck, but I'm not complaining. It's close to seven and I'm hungry and horny.

"Hey." I kiss her on one cheek and then the other as her jasmine perfume floats in, announcing her presence before she steps into the Carrara marble foyer.

Alessia is a beautiful woman with high cheekbones, a fair complexion, blue eyes, and honey-colored hair. I'm sure my mother would be thrilled if we married as she comes from an old Florentine family.

In my world, status is based on money first, followed second by the fact we are all Florentine, born and raised in families who have lived in Florence for generations. We have our own dialect and traditions here which set us apart from other Italian families.

"How are you?" Sliding her thin arms around my neck, the pressure makes its way through my shirt.

I can't say I mind the feel of her smooth skin on my neck. My lips descend on hers in a passionate kiss. It's instinctive in nature, part of the crude and ruthless code of being a single, dangerous man.

"Fine." I break away and murmur against her, "Hungry?"

"Hmm, only for you," she purrs, surrendering her lips to me again.

I play with her pale pink luscious lips, and if I liked catnip, I'd be enthralled. Alas, I'm not, but I can play the game, tugging and releasing to create a pace for our sexual desires as I feel her melt under me.

With one arm wrapped around her back, I pull her hips into mine so hard her fake boobs jiggle as if they're real, and I feel naughty as I press my hard cock against her stomach. She has no idea what I'm capable of, and I will keep it that way. Someday, she'll be someone's wife—a nice man who comes home on schedule. I picture her with one child and never working.

"Dante," she murmurs against my ear, and her soft breath passes like a light breeze, light enough to excite me even more.

My cock is like a racehorse, anxious to get us out of the starting gate and waiting to take a long, hard ride. I wrap my other arm around her so she can feel my hardness pulsating against her pussy. She knows I'm ready for her, and I'm not very patient with things I know are mine.

"Upstairs," I command, releasing her and pointing in the general direction. She dutifully turns, and her Gucci heels make a soft tat sound on the marble steps as she makes her way to the second floor.

I follow her at a distance, so I can take in the sway of her hips as she walks saucily up the winding staircase and dances her fingers along the wrought-iron handrail as she makes her way up the steps she knows well, probably too well. I really need to cut her loose, but I keep her around as she's my only link to a normal world, affection, and sex.

I pull off my shirt and loosen my belt, taking two steps at a time as she peers over her left shoulder to see where I am. Seeing me behind her, she takes the steps faster, giggling and trying to stay ahead of me. I capture her at the top of the stairs, and she squeals as I swing her through the air and set her on the landing. We race to my room, and when we reach the doorway, I scoop her up and toss her on the bed.

"Lose the panties."

Alessia flashes me a saucy grin and pulls up her dress to show me she's not wearing any panties, then flicks off her heels. They sail through the air before making a thunk on the hard floor.

The house was modernized years ago, and I have air conditioning units to cool individual rooms, but tonight, the summer air is cool enough for my shutters to be open. Sweet-smelling wisteria fills the room, invited in on the breeze. Yet one more reason to live at the top of the mountain.

I drop my pants and boxers and crawl toward her. My cock is

hard, enough of these childish games, enough foreplay, my needs are basic, and I need immediate stress relief. And she knows it.

She places one hand on my chest as her other hand grabs my pulsating cock and tugs as I let out a quiet moan. She slides her hands across the ripples of muscles in my shoulders and biceps like she's never felt them before.

I insert two fingers into her and roughly move them back and forth, making sure she's ready before I pull them out and enter her, taking her hard and fast.

She gasps, and the look of surprise on her face is priceless as she moves with me. She clings to my torso as I'm on the edge of ripping her apart, I'm so intent on rubbing one out in her. I'm not concerned if she comes or not—I have to remain in control of myself and detached.

She moans and arches her back as I explode inside her, and after a brief pause, I roll off. I lie there with my eyes closed, enjoying the moment when my phone rings. It's as if someone waited until I climaxed.

"Pronto," I answer and listen. I respond and tell them to do what is necessary, then hang up.

My stomach growls at me.

"You want some dinner? I have some of Mama's Bolognese Sauce."

"Sure." She sits up, using the bed sheet to wipe away the proof of our fuck. I pull on my pants, going commando, and head downstairs.

I haven't eaten and I'm fucking starving as I pull a bowl of sauce from the refrigerator and a saucepan from a rack on the wall. I use the gas stove to warm the sauce and use a double boiler to rewarm the pasta.

She enters the kitchen. "You seem preoccupied."

"Yeah, always. What's new?"

"More than usual," she presses. "Anything I can do to help?"

I lean toward her as she retrieves silverware out of a drawer near me and give her a light kiss on the lips. "No, but thanks."

She shrugs her shoulders, accustomed to my cold nature, and sets the table, examining the label on the wine on the table before opening it to let it breathe.

"Good year for Chianti," she remarks.

"Hmm, yes it was," I mutter absently, as I recall retrieving it from the wine cellar yesterday. This particular bottle should air for three hours.

Shit.

This is one of those instances where a tiny bit of planning would have been nice. Now, I will be drinking an expensive wine when it's not at its peak.

I fill our plates with food and apologize for the lack of appetizers as we sit across from each other at the kitchen table. This is where I feel the most comfortable. The dining room is too formal for anything less than six or more people.

I think I like it here because it reminds me of visiting Grandpa growing up and how Grandma would spend the day in the kitchen, making pasta from scratch using a crank-handled pasta machine. She did all the dishes by hand too, even though they had a dishwasher.

We eat in relative silence, making light conversation when it's warranted. When we finish, I whisk the plates away, soaking them in a sink full of dishwater.

"Let me help," she offers.

"No, you're my guest, but I really need to get back to work."

Her face falls in disappointment, which tells me she anticipated more. Of course, she wants more.

It's just for a few seconds, then she recovers her look of indifference. She knows she must remain so in order for me to keep seeing her. But the time it took for her to recover was a few seconds too many.

I know she will be hurt when I no longer call.

# CHAPTER 6

## DANTE

*I* can't sleep and lie awake replaying the events of the day, then hearing the phone conversation in my head. I'm not happy I lost a few men, and I bet it's a message from Conti, the prick. I want to end him for what he's started. The man has no ethics and no boundaries when it comes to what's off-limits.

I'm no babe in the woods. I realize that there are no rules in organized crime anymore, and in that respect, I'm more like my father than I would like to admit. I criticized him for doing the same thing I'm doing now, and we lost ground in the south to Conti because of it. I will not lose one more inch of my turf.

Maybe the real reason I toss and turn in my empty bed is my decision to kidnap Juliet. She's more than just a hostage—she's our largest rival's daughter, which makes her an asset. Even if Conti doesn't care about her, once her name gets out, there will be a feeding frenzy between all the syndicated crime factions who have a beef with Conti. So, he has more to gain by keeping his love child under wraps.

But how can I protect her? The best way to do that would be to have her marry a member of my family. Then she would be a common element shared by two of the most famous and powerful

34

warring mafia clans. That could work, but it could also backfire. If the Contis renege on their word, she will be directly in the crosshairs. She could get hurt.

I turn onto one side, then the other, then I roll onto my back. Nope, still can't sleep. I stare at the ceiling and feel my cock harden under the silk sheets. I look down at what reminds me of a lone tent in the middle of an empty desert, kinda like my life.

Fuck me.

I'm in the middle of kidnapping some asshole's bastard and this is what my fucking cock wants? What am I thinking? I know not to mix business with pleasure. If the guys get wind I have feelings for her, even just the hots for her, it gives them leverage, and that I cannot afford. Besides, there's my rule to never fall in love. A woman, a wife, a family is always a weakness in this business. I'm counting on Juliet being Conti's weakness, so it wouldn't be smart to turn around and make her my own Achilles heel.

I get up, throw on some boxers, and walk to Juliet's room. The guard nods and I twist the antique knob and crack the door open. She's sleeping peacefully in my dress shirt, and it warms my cold heart.

Who am I kidding? How can I marry her off to one of my brothers when I want her myself? My cock is hard every time I'm near her. I get a whiff of her lilac scent, faint but fragrant. I close the door, satisfied she's safe.

I'm selfish and used to getting what I want regardless of the consequences. But this is no time to want something that I can't have like this woman to warm my heart and bed, a good woman who has a normal life, a life that any father would want for his daughter. No, it would be an impossible situation.

It's going to be tricky, a birth father and an adoptive father in the same equation. Families are problematic at best, and the Contis are notorious for their ruthlessness. They could just decide to kill her and get rid of the liability. I need to factor that into the equation and make sure it doesn't happen, or the years it

ZOE BETH GELLER

took me to find her will just have been a colossal waste of time and money.

Whatever it takes, I need to resolve this before I lose any more men to Conti's messages written in blood and sent with bullets. Maybe he doesn't realize I'm the reason there have been no wars since my dad died. Well, he's gonna find out soon enough.

How dare he treat me like I'm nothing because I'm young and because I'm not his famiglia? We're not backing off... we're moving in. With that attitude in mind, I crawl back into bed and fall asleep before the birds start their chirping.

The sun is higher than usual when I wake up and quickly throw on a pair of old jeans I fish out of the laundry hamper. Anticipating Juliet is already up, I head downstairs to check on her.

Fresh-pressed coffee greets my nose as I reach the first floor. Walking into the kitchen, I see Juliet standing with her back to me, still wearing my dress shirt. She reaches up to get a cup off the shelf, and the shirt rides up, showing me a glimpse of her bare ass. My cock twitches and I want to bend her over the marble counter and take what is mine.

"What are you doing?" I bark, angry because I'm developing feelings for her and she's getting to me emotionally. We barely know each other and I'm acting possessive.

"Making coffee, would you like an espresso or cappuccino?" She turns around and blinks at me mildly.

I can see the outline of her hard nipples through the thin fabric of the shirt. I clench my fists to stop myself from mauling her and curse myself for not giving her a robe to wear instead.

"Espresso," I reply with tight lips, giving in to my favorite routine in the morning, except for fucking, because I'm tongue-tied and horny.

No other woman has ever driven me crazy like this. How am I supposed to not fuck someone I'm so sexually attracted to? I'm reminded of my vow to remain single seeing how one woman can play with my cock, mess with my head, and pull my heartstrings all at the same time.

Christ. We haven't even fucked. Once that happens, I'm really screwed.

It's not just her ass made for grabbing that has my head spinning. She has a sweetness about her I find irresistible, even if I'm not worthy of it. I mean, look at the marks on her wrists from the zip ties yesterday. She didn't deserve that. The regret at hurting her is a first for me. I've never thought twice about inflicting pain to get what I want.

Maybe the fact I'm using her to punish my nemesis is driving my excitement. Whatever it is, I need to keep my focus on building an empire, not building a romance.

"We're going shopping today. You can't walk around dressed like that. The minidress you had on yesterday was cute but looks like something your American friend would wear. You are Italian, and you need to wear classier stuff."

She doesn't answer. Instead, she takes a sip of espresso and questions me with her eyes, one perfectly sleek eyebrow raised. She probably doesn't think I'm serious. How does one go from being tied to a chair one day to high-end shopping the next? I get it. I'd be skeptical too.

"Yeah, I know. Men hate shopping, but I can't have you running around half-naked. Besides, you need to be able to go outside and use the grounds. There's a heated infinity pool off the living room." I all but chastise her over the fact I'm horny as hell every time I see her, not to mention her shapely legs and pert breasts. I surmise they would fit comfortably in my large hands.

"A pool?" Her surprise reminds me how unusual it is in Italy for there to be a pool in the backyard. Now she's getting an idea where she is, somewhere only the mega-wealthy can afford to live. But she still has no idea how close she is to Florence. To keep her from figuring it out, we're going to head in the opposite direction, to places she's hopefully never seen before.

My personal tailor gave me a list of cities outside Florence where we can shop for designer clothing, and it just so happens we have an errand to run in Milan anyway. I don't want to return to Rome just yet, so we're going to need the jet.

"We need to get you something other than my shirt to wear," I repeat with a wave of my hand as if it's nothing unusual. She leans in to set a cup of espresso in front of me, and rather than averting my eyes, I admire the view and then I grumble under my breath when I pop a boner.

I can't breathe, swallow, or blink as I watch her full breasts and pink nipples rub and harden against the fabric of my six-hundred-dollar Dolce & Gabbana shirt. If I didn't know better, I'd swear she was flirting with me, but that's not like her. She's not flashy or trashy. If anything, she's unassuming and sweet.

My cock swells and I'm uncomfortable as it strains against my jeans and I'm dying to pound one off inside her right now, but I can't bend her over this table in front of the guards. No, this will have to be planned. An overnight stay in Milan is just what I need. Great views, out of sight, sounds like a solid plan. I'm impressed I came up with the idea so quickly.

God, get it together, I chastise myself. I like it better when I'm in control of the situation, and right now, I definitely do not feel in control. Maybe all this serving me coffee half-naked is a setup, a ploy to get me to lower my guard. Flirting leads to fucking, and fucking leads to mistakes.

I down my espresso quickly and leave abruptly.

I feel her eyes on my back, but I have things to do, and for now, keeping my mind occupied is the only way I can keep it off her pussy.

\* \* \*

I have Riccardo bring me more espresso as I reply to emails on my phone while he gets the jet ready for a day out, maybe even an overnight trip. I have him pack a bag for me while I sit in a cushioned chair by the pool, a pool I rarely use. I should probably swim more. I'm thirty and don't want to lose what God was kind enough to bless me with as I eat anything I want and I'm still thin.

I use the inside gym three to four times a week to keep my chest and arms not just looking good but strong enough to fight if I need to. I played football in college, but these days, I don't have time for organized sports, nor would it be wise for me to do so in any case. Adding swimming to my routine might be a good idea.

And the anticipation of seeing Juliet in a swimsuit is just the motivation I need.

Riccardo sits beside me while I text pictures of Juliet's birth certificate to Conti. I tell him we have her and if the hits on my men don't cease, she'll be on his conscience.

Three dots show up on my phone, then nothing.

"I imagine he needs a minute to think," I say vaguely, but my worried face conveys what my words don't.

"We'll wait to see what his next move is, boss. He might just keep it to himself."

My eyebrows furrow. "He's sitting on a powder keg. He can't keep it a secret. It's out now, and he knows we can use it at any time." And for the first time in my life, I think about my captive as a human being and not a number in an equation. It dawns on me I may have jeopardized Juliet's life.

Riccardo takes a long draw on his vape pen. "True. He knows you'll use it, too."

"Exactly. Well, we'll let him think on it. I'm sure we'll hear back soon enough." For the first time since becoming the don, I'm nervous about which way Conti will go. He's a mean fuck. I'd hate to be tortured by him.

Riccardo nods and gets up, indicating we need to be going.

"I'll be with you in a few," I add, enjoying the view of the pool for just a few more minutes as the morning breeze moves through the leaves of the olive trees, creating a small ripple on the water's surface. The sun warms my skin and for once, I'm relaxed.

I need to shower and shave. It's weird having another person in the house all the time. Juliet's here because Conti will be less likely to fly off into a violent rage if he knows his daughter is not sleeping on the floor in some abandoned warehouse. He might be more pissed if he knew she was in my house. However, I hadn't considered my privacy when I planned to take a hostage.

I know he got one over on my old man, but he's wrong if he thinks I'm cut from the same cloth. I can spend the rest of my life thinking up ways to make him miserable.

I make my way upstairs and pass Riccardo, who is delivering jeans and a shirt to Juliet's room. He said she asked for some art supplies, so I told him to buy whatever she wants. It will help keep her occupied.

Riccardo is holding onto her phone to monitor who is trying to reach her so we don't raise suspicion. It's amazing how easy it is to pose as someone when you're in possession of their cell phone.

I chuck my jeans, turn on the taps, and step under the shower head made to resemble a rainstorm. The side jets kick in, and I close my eyes and imagine what it would be like to have Juliet pressed up against the glass in this shower with my tongue in . . .

Cretino! I don't have time for this. Turning off the water, I dry off, shave, and put on a suit suitable for a day of shopping.

I'm already sitting up front in the Rover when Juliet arrives and gets in without complaint. No doubt because the guard glued to her side has a gun under his jacket.

I turn around and see her eyes wide with amazement as she gazes up at the front of the estate for the first time. I hear a tiny gasp escape her luscious lips—lips I can't wait to claim.

# CHAPTER 7

JULIET

*I* love the energetic vibe of living in Florence. Not to say I don't love relaxing at home in the country, but I prefer city life. I never would have been happy had I stayed at home and not sought my own life.

I'm over living in the dorms, but at the same time, the cost of living is high, and I don't know how I can afford to get an apartment.

Obviously, I'd have to share it with someone and get a job, which would suck. I have loads of experience waitressing, and I'd easily find a job with all the tourists. But I'm stubborn. I don't want to take time away from my art.

I work until my wrists are sore and my tired eyes are just slits, making tiny strokes with my charcoal pencil as I work on yet another project. My sketch pad is filling up, and to me, that's a success. I live, eat, and breathe art, and walking around Florence, where it's embedded in every aspect of our life, is amazing.

The night rain brings humidity and I turn on the small unit to give us cold air to make the small dorm bearable. Hotels here usually have power to the air connected to the light switch and the temperature gauges locked under a plexiglass cover because electricity is so expensive, but thankfully, our university hasn't caught on to that idea yet. I know it's coming. Until then, I'll enjoy the cool air.

I sigh, unable to get the face right on the sketch I'm working on. It's so much easier getting the angles of the jawline right when I have a picture to follow. I'm not good at imagining faces and drawing them.

I finish penciling in the outline and Ava walks over, fresh out of the shower with her hair up in a towel.

"Whoa, that's the dude from yesterday. Mr. Sexy Eyes."

"What?"

"Remember the hottie standing next to the dean yesterday? That's him," she squeals. "I think you have a crush."

"Thuff." I make a disapproving sound to convey to her just how I feel about it. "No way," I point to the guy on my desk, "that's not him."

She snickers.

I examine the sketch again.

"Fuck."

"See, told ya."

"I've never done that before. I can't make up faces. I mean, I didn't even really talk to him or anything. How can that be?"

"Maybe he's your guy?"

"He was dark and mysterious for sure." And I'm not sure what to do with my sketch now. To be honest, I'm a bit freaked out.

"Relax." She takes the towel off her hair and bends forward, flipping her hair over her head, and using the towel to scrunch it into curls without it frizzing. "You'll probably never see him again. I wonder who he is. I mean, if he knows the dean, he's got to be somebody, right?"

"Probably." She's new here and doesn't understand money has a way of fluttering around Florence since the beginning of time without any questions asked.

My mind drifts back to the courtyard, remembering I was rather quiet, even for me.

"I wonder who you are, Mr. Sexy Eyes," I say as I hold the paper at arm's length to take in with a fresh look. "He really was incredibly good-looking."

"Oh, hell yes," Ava agrees as she flips herself upright and lets her damp hair fall naturally around her face. "I'd do him."

"Ava!" I shouldn't be shocked. It seems like nowadays people are lonely and it's getting harder to meet nice guys to date. The internet has made it easier to meet people, but not necessarily the right people.

"What? We have this game in the States, called Marry, Shag, Kill."

My jaw drops. It sounds so barbaric.

"We don't really kill them, it's just a silly game," she adds after she hears me gasp in surprise.

This college experience is surely broadening my world experience, but I don't think it's in ways my parents would appreciate.

"Wow, okay, so the guy yesterday?"

"Definitely shag," she decides as she fluffs up her curls with her fingertips and looks at herself in the full-length mirror. "Yes, fuckable, many times over." She turns to me. "You?"

"Oh, I wouldn't know, I've only been with a few guys."

"Wow, that's unusual. I mean, there was a time in the States when girls wore promise rings, vowing to remain virgins until they got married. But let me tell you, I'm so fucking glad that shit was done before I became a teenager."

I've never heard of any of this, and it reinforces my notion Americans are a little... different.

"Wow, who promises such things? Teenagers? Really?"

"Well, each generation is different. I'm just glad it wasn't my generation because I love sex. And speaking of sex, I have a lunch date with that hottie in our afternoon class."

Of course, she does; meanwhile, I'm left alone again. I thought he was hot too, I'd do him. I had a few hookups last year, but the well has been dry for some time. I'm not sure why the hookups didn't lead to more. Maybe it's just the fact that Italian men have a short attention span and they're always on to the next conquest. Plus, with all the foreign women coming here now, they see us as plain and ordinary, like vanilla-flavored gelato. Why settle for vanilla when you can have a different flavor every night?

Ava pulls out some clothes and lays two outfits on her bed, trying to choose.

"Where are you going for lunch?"

"He's showing me around the Uffizi, then we're eating in the café at the top."

"Nice," I agree with envy, "the view from there is amazing."

"I hope so, but to be honest, I think the view of my tour guide will be all I'm looking at."

I make my way to her bed. "The outfit on the right, red is for passion."

She surprises me with a hug. "You're the best."

"No problem," I reply, deciding I need to find something to do today, like finding some new clothes.

Ava has so many cute clothes; my wardrobe pales in comparison. Maybe if I got some newer styles, I'd have the college guys asking me out. It wouldn't hurt to window shop.

Yeah, I'll go out and look in the fancy shops today, and if I like something, I'll put it on my credit card. Then I'll have to get a job to pay it off. I know it's wrong, but what better motivation than to shop first? Besides, I doubt I'll find anything that looks nearly as cute on me as the red minidress Ava is wearing, the one that screams, 'Make love to me now.'

Ava turns so I can zip up the back of her dress, then turns back again so I can see.

"You look fantastic."

"Thanks. So, what are you doing today?"

"I think I'll check out the clothing shops. Standing next to you makes me feel as plain as... I don't know. Plain."

Ava stares at me, her mouth agape. "Oh my God, don't say that! You're gorgeous, your hair is so dark and shiny." She runs her fingers through the ends of my hair. "You're like two sizes smaller than me and can rock a pair of skinny jeans. I can't even get them over my ass. You just need to look at men like you want them. You don't really look at guys, you know, look in their eyes."

"I don't feel like they see me, for me," I falter, and she's right. I have a bad habit of avoiding men and I don't understand it. I like guys.

"It's easy to fix. Don't go bankrupt today."

"I know a few places and they aren't tourist traps." I can't withhold my grin, conveying this is my home away from home.

"Yeah, yeah." She smiles as she sits, applying makeup in front of a mirror with special lighting.

"We'll see. I might get a job. I saved up a lot working at my parents' restaurant, but I'm running out of money, and I don't want my parents to buy my clothes and stuff."

"That's good of you. Where I'm from, kids expect it."

"Lots here do too, but I'm not that way." I close my sketchpad and put my supplies back in their boxes.

I put on a pair of low heels, so I feel sexier in my jeans, before grabbing my purse to hold essentials and sliding my cell phone inside next to my small wallet.

She looks up from applying the lip liner. "Have fun, I'll see ya tonight... probably."

"Have a good time." I scoot out the door.

The streets still look wet from the rain, and noisy Vespas zip around like flies at a picnic. They're still the cheapest form of personal transportation, and I swear they outnumber the people.

I think about where I'd like to work and wonder if I'd get a discount working in a clothing store. Then again, most sell high-end designers who, even with a discount, are still unaffordable.

Maybe I'll fill out applications at a few restaurants if I see they're hiring.

The tweeting birds mock me. It's mating season for them, and it seems to be the same for everyone except me. Mr. Sexy Eyes comes to mind, and I wonder if I'll ever see him again. He looked older, yeah, definitely older. Maybe that's my problem, it suddenly occurs to me. I'm looking to date men my own age, and maybe that's a mistake.

I need to open up more and expand my horizons. I'm guilty of looking at guys who are goofing off and I feel like I'm their mother, not their peer. It probably wouldn't hurt to smile more and wear a shorter dress. You're only young once and my legs won't look this good forever.

# CHAPTER 8

## DANTE

*M*y bedroom shutters are fully open as I stand at the window and gaze at the olive grove behind my house. It's still early, but the morning is warming up and there is no breeze, so it's going to be a hot day. The windows will need to be closed soon and that's why I'm so happy to have Rosario, who lives in the tiny house at the back, to take care of everything for me, especially when I'm not here.

Riccardo will be here soon to drive me to the airport. I love having my own jet. We could take the train, but let's face it, I'm me and I like to get in and out quickly. Plus, I don't have time to waste. And of course, it's safer.

Riccardo shows up with a hot cappuccino, which I gladly accept. I will be carrying a briefcase with numbers inside to show Conti. I just hope this isn't a setup to even old scores. I have men on the ground who have overheard that becoming a grandfather has softened him up a bit. The jury is out on that, but how safe can I really be outside of Tuscany and central Italy where we are in control? Even on a good day and during good times, yeah, I can walk the streets, but I can't be caught mingling with underworld figures. That would risk a strike.

I understand. I would do the same. It's usually not personal when someone needs to be handled. With a don, well, a warning message would be sent first. Maybe a capo would suffer an untimely death. It's not like we don't know what the other families are up to or planning to do. The criminal world has its food chain, and everyone knows someone. If not, we have ways to make them talk.

It's like office politics, but the consequences if you aren't good at the game can be a lot more permanent.

"Blue, um, power suit," Riccardo busts my chops, and I wouldn't have it any other way. He's drinking his black coffee and wearing a gray suit. The salt-and-pepper color in his beard makes him look distinguished for a man his age. His light hazel-green eyes are watching me over his paper cup, amused.

"What? Should I be wearing black?"

"Your funeral." He smirks.

"You fuck." I give him a half-cocked grin. "What, you want to pick out a pine wood box as well?"

"Oh hell no. God, if you pull this off, you'll be like the king of kings."

I tuck in my white dress shirt and run my hand over the stiff collar before I slide into my matching jacket. It's easier to wear than carry. I pick up the black briefcase with my free hand, and we're out the door.

"Maybe I'm dead already." I give him my best evil look before we break out in what might be called a nervous chuckle.

Riccardo opens my door, and I slide into the Rover. I like to drive my sports cars for fun, but the mundane work stuff, not so much. I hate traffic, and I find myself cursing all the time, so it's probably better for my health Riccardo drives. Plus, I don't carry a weapon.

Riccardo carries his old man's revolver under his jacket, which I appreciate, especially on a day like today. But he's even-tempered, so I don't have to worry about him flying off the handle in a moment of crisis.

We're at the airport and walking onto the tarmac in under forty-five minutes. The airport is near Prato, a smaller suburb outside of Florence. It's so old, only smaller planes land here, but I prefer it this way. It's safer and time-efficient.

The flight takes no time at all, so I mix myself a Bloody Mary on the way just because I'm thirsty, and tomato juice is considered part of breakfast. It's a fruit only red and not orange, so why the fuck not?

When we deplane in Rome, my Ferragamo loafers hit the hot tarmac, and I regret not arranging this trip in winter. Then again, we'd be in a monsoon because wintertime is when the city gets lots of rain, so pick your poison.

We have a limo service waiting and make our way to the Mercedes van for the forty-five-minute drive to the meet. The closer we get to the Colosseum, the more congested the traffic gets. As bad as traffic is in Florence, Rome traffic is insane. Craning my head around, I am finally able to see the back part of the beautiful ruin as we circle from the lower end and wind up the hill on a long bend, wrapping around it like Cleopatra's deadly asp. I hope I'm not about to get bitten myself.

We arrive at the elegant Hotel Palazzo Manfredi and take an elevator to the terrace. The doors open, and with the sun directly overhead, the view of the Colosseum is breathtaking. The terrace is surrounded by glass windows and covered with a pale awning to let the sunlight in, but keeps out the rain.

We spot our table immediately as I make out the face of Conti himself, surrounded by four others, younger, in their thirties and forties, no doubt his sons or capos. I approach with Riccardo on my heels, showing respect.

I extend my hand to Gio Conti. His eyes are dark and brooding, and I can tell he'll not willingly go for anything I'm about to propose. But he'll learn submission before I'm done with him. I'm like a dog with a steak bone that way.

"Hello, Dante," he says politely but coolly as he gives my hand a tight grip. We look each other in the eye, and neither of us flinches. It's like we're kids playing a game of chicken. And here I had hoped he would be wiser at his age and stop making everything a challenge or an exercise in one-upmanship.

Riccardo suggests we sit, and the others follow suit. Conti doesn't introduce his people, only one, who is his son, Mario. My extra bodyguards are standing at our backs, looking a bit conspicuous, but that's how it's done. No one else is on the terrace. It's just us.

It's the first time I've met Conti in person. He oozes the sliminess of the criminal world and I see in an instant that while he might dress up, he will never lose the cutthroat vibe of a desperate kid on the street willing to do anything, even screw over his daughter, if it means he'll be a don for all eternity. He loves power and games, perfect for the life he's chosen. But as part of the older crowd, he's about to get left behind as he doesn't fit our modern image or brand anymore. I wonder if he realizes it.

"I'll get right down to it. We would like to use the Port of Civitavecchia to move goods, and in return, we are prepared to offer you this." I slide a paper toward him, showing the breakdown and his percentage.

He doesn't even look at the paper. "No. I don't have to let anyone in my port. I control it, it's my lifeline, why would I share?"

"Don Conti, I promise you, we're just bringing in goods. We won't infringe upon your territory. You'll make more money, and everyone is happy."

He downs a scotch and slams the rocks glass on the table. "I don't need to make anyone happy but my wife," he replies, drawing the words out slowly with a bit of a huff before ceremoniously jabbing his elbow into his son's ribs.

He has no idea I know his dirty secret. He's had a long series of extramarital affairs, and I suspect he won't be able to buy his wife's forgiveness with another expensive piece of jewelry if she ever finds out what I know.

My lips never part, making my smile undetectable.

I order a couple of scotches for Riccardo and myself and we exchange pleasantries until we make excuses about having other business to attend to, which is a lie, and he knows it. This is all a formality. To be honest, I didn't expect anything less of him given his reputation and prior dealings with my family. But how far will he go to resist our past agreement he reneged on?

I'm a patient man in general, which is a good character trait for a don, but I have my limitations. He's been screwing us over for years and spreading lies about my family. If it goes so far that I have his daughter at my house? Fuck yeah, then it would be personal. His lies have been pissing me off for years, and nothing would please me more than to get the revenge my old man couldn't.

I collect my briefcase, make a small half bow to show respect to Conti, and we leave with our guards following in their black business suits and Polaroid sunglasses, looking like American Secret Service agents I've seen in the movies.

"Hmm, interesting," Riccardo muses aloud as we make our way toward the elevator.

I quiet him with a glance. We still have to be careful what we say. We don't know where all his men are, and some could be the wait staff. I wouldn't put it past him, because I would do the same if I wanted intel.

I turn to Riccardo after the elevator doors close and sense it's safe to speak. "He's smart for keeping the port, so he can squeeze anyone, even if he's in business with them. I don't relish doing business with him, but since we can't use the port on the other coast due to the earthquake last year, he's got us over a barrel, and he knows it. But like I said, let him enjoy it. We have the one thing no one else has... and he loves his wife," I say with a sardonic tone. "You do know how much he loves his wife, right?"

Riccardo smiles. "Yeah, I picked up on that. Too bad he's never stopped fucking around on her. Imagine a man his age with a—how young is the latest one? A twenty-five-year-old mistress?"

"Yeah, everyone knows that. We, however, have the holy grail." I finally smile, showing my straight pearly white teeth as we climb into our waiting limo.

"Oh yeah, we do." Riccardo texts the guys back home to make sure they are still sitting on the girl and not raising any eyebrows as they do so. The last thing we need is a fuck-up.

It's getting too hot to wear this jacket outside, but the cold air from the vents keeps me comfortable in the limo. I'm no global warming expert, but I swear the summer heat starts earlier every year.

I decided today wasn't a defeat but pretty much what I expected. Conti is cocky. I'm good at chess, and this was my opening gambit. It's a long-distance run, not a sprint.

Getting off the plane in Prato, Riccardo wants to eat dinner, so we stop at the piazza in Fiesole and eat at my favorite local Italian restaurant. I love that families are still hanging on to their restaurants even though we have chains like American sub shops and Irish pubs popping up like weeds in a garden.

When it comes to food, I never skimp on quality. I would have preferred to eat near the university as I'm curious about Juliet, but I can't risk being seen again. It's bad enough I went there earlier this week.

Hot rolls are brought to our table, and I break off a piece, dip it in olive oil with seasoning, and let it melt in my mouth. I didn't realize how hungry I was until I started eating, but now, I feel like having two meals. The antipasti arrives, followed at a leisurely pace by the entrée of veal and a side of pasta. I eat until I'm satisfied and content. My day is complete.

But I can't get Juliet's dark eyes off my mind, and I don't know why. She's so young, early twenties if she's a day, and way too innocent for a man in his prime surrounded by guards and living the life I do.

\* \* \*

The next day is Sunday, and I head to Mama's house for family day. She spends the entire day preparing dinner with the help of her long-time friend and maid, Isabelle. Mama always says we are her reason for living, especially since she's alone.

Mama is adamant about everyone attending Sunday dinner, and trust me, it's not worth crossing her on that. Given that I live alone, and Riccardo is the only person in the world I interact with outside of a quick lay, spending Sundays with family isn't really so bad.

I pull up to the large circular stone driveway. This old Tuscan house is too large for her to take care of, even when Dad was alive, but we all know better than to even think of suggesting she move somewhere else.

I walk in, and Mama rushes to kiss me on one cheek, then the other. She immediately starts rattling on about the food and how she doesn't think she made enough for everyone, even though she's never once run out of food. She's wearing an apron just like when we were kids, even though she's always had a housekeeper.

"Relax, it's fine." I kiss her on both cheeks before she takes off for the kitchen in the back of the house.

"It's a nice night. Everything is set up outside," she says, pointing at a long table on the patio as she scuttles away.

I walk out back and greet my brothers, Sal and Marchello. I guess after three sons, Mama gave up on having a girl.

Isabelle has been with the family forever. She brings out a platter loaded with slices of fresh mozzarella and vine-ripened tomatoes, decorated with basil leaves, and drizzled with a balsamic glaze made from what's left over in the wine barrels.

After I greet my brothers, I notice the table is missing someone.

"Where's Carla?" I ask, turning to Sal as he pours us each a glass of wine.

He shrugs his shoulders dismissively. "Women. She's upset. She heard I kissed her best friend."

"Did you?"

"Eh, I'm Italian, aren't I?"

I knock him upside the head lightly, not to hurt him but to still make my point. "You're an idiot."

He looks back at me innocently. "What was I supposed to do? Carla said I didn't kiss well. I had to defend my honor."

"What honor?" Marchello pipes up, taking a sip of wine.

"What about you, Dante? God, do you ever get laid? You never have a girlfriend. I'm tired of Mama nagging me with a million questions."

"You know I'll never get married. I have limits on how long I see someone before that's that, on to the next one. It keeps my head in the business. As long as I'm in charge of myself and stick to my rules, no one else will share my life."

"Yeah. Dad never had time to play with us. And then there was that time we had to leave town in the middle of the night . . ." Marchello's voice trails off.

I raise my glass. "To happier times."

"Salute," my brothers say in unison.

An evening breeze caresses my face, and for some strange reason, I'm reminded of Juliet. I find myself wondering what she would be like in bed and berate myself for even thinking about her that way.

Riccardo joins us under the canopy of the umbrella pines, and my brothers acknowledge him before the two of us walk out of their earshot.

He asks, "Ready for the plan?"

"Sure. I'll stumble onto campus tomorrow, invite her out, and then we'll nab her."

"Then we'll blindfold her and drive all over, so she won't know where she is," he continues.

"Perfect. With any luck, Conti will cave in short order. We'll get what we want, and he'll get his daughter back. Although, after meeting him, I don't think he will leave us alone even after we let her go. His love of greed and natural flair for sickening and unpredictable behavior makes him dangerous."

"You think we need to take care of her? What did your consigliere say? Did he approve?"

"Nicolo said it's a calculated risk. The man is a known psychopath who instills fear in his own men by reputation, imagine his presence in front of them. I can't imagine being around such a whack job. I hate to bring an innocent girl into this. It's not her fault who her father is. I think it's our best play to get what we want. We'll be prepared with some sort of contingency plan." I hope this satisfies my siblings' concerns over another war with the twisted Conti family.

I don't know how I overlooked this huge detail. There's nothing to stop Conti from pursuing us even if he gives into our demands. He'll be angry we went after family, even if it's family he thought he had kept hidden from his enemies.

"I wanted to smack that smirk off his face yesterday. He truly is insufferable. Maybe we'll have an impromptu wedding. After all, I do have two brothers who need wives," I state, "and it would get Mama out of my personal life."

"That would get Mama off your back for a minute," Sal chuckles.

"Maybe a minute," I agree. "Not much more."

Being the oldest puts so much more shit on my shoulders. It's not just the business, it's taking care of Mama and my brothers and our employees. This business with Conti has me worried about what will happen to Juliet once we set the plan in motion. His stubbornness and greed have forced my hand. Not that I need an excuse for using force when needed. No one in my family will ever call me weak.

"Beautiful view from here," Riccardo looks out over the valley below. It's a choice piece of real estate for sure.

Cherry blossoms are in bloom, and the sweetness wafts up from Mama's orchard below. The pink petals are colorful against the dark bark of the tree limbs, and I'm reminded of a young woman's succulent lips once again.

Thankfully, my thoughts are interrupted before I get a hard-on fantasizing about someone who doesn't know anything about me but my name.

"Mangia! Mangia!" Mama calls us over to eat.

The dinner table is long, and the trees make a perfect canopy over it. During the day, they provide shade, and as night begins to fall, the lights strung in the trees turn on, creating the perfect ambiance for a perfect meal.

The bread is fresh from the bakery around the corner, and the meat is from the butcher shop Mama's gone to forever. I remember as a small boy standing next to her with my nose against the glass case and seeing fresh ground beef in a bowl next to steaks and sausages. Next to it, the veal and chicken are on skewers ready for grilling, like Mama used to make when Babbo was home early enough to eat with us. Looking up, the cured meats hang from the ceiling, the salami, pepperoni, and my favorite, prosciutto.

I'm at the head of the table with Riccardo at my right and Mama on my left.

"Ma, you made enough food for an army," I protest, and of course, she waves me off like it was nothing when I know she spent all day in the kitchen.

"I'm just so happy everyone is here. When are you going to bring a nice girl to dinner? You never bring any girlfriends to dinner. I'm your mother, I want to see you with a girlfriend, Dante. It's not good being alone. Trust me, I know."

And now, Sunday is complete.

# CHAPTER 9

## JULIET

*A*va was out all day yesterday and is totally enthralled with her date, which, from what I can gather, included a trip back to his apartment for some hot, sweaty sex. Now, she is in my room looking at the clothes I bought on my mini spree. I'm glad to see she approves of them.

"I'm in a dry spell. I hope these clothes help."

Ava picks up the short minidress I bought at a trendy but not-too-expensive boutique. It fit perfectly, so I had to buy it. I put it on my charge card and figure I'll get a job in the next few weeks as I managed to fill out a few applications on my way to the shop.

"This is adorable," she exclaims.

That's probably her code for 'it's so unlike you to wear something like this', but I'll take it as a compliment because I can't remember the last time I had one.

It's Sunday and the church bells are chiming as mass is starting around the corner. It's one of the few things that hasn't changed in Italy. Thank God something has stayed the same, even if these days the bell ringers have been replaced by electrical timers. It's a comforting, familiar sound.

I'm also sure it's one of the last things tourists will forget when they get on the plane bound for home, laden with their physical souvenirs.

"I don't know why I bought this dress, Ava. I have nowhere to wear it."

"So, we'll have to go out to a club!"

"All right. We have to be careful though, they can be dangerous."

"So I've heard, but we'll be together."

"Yeah," I reply. I realize I haven't been out in months, and I need to kick up my heels.

"Well, I'm grabbing a coffee with my date from yesterday, so I'll be back in a few hours. Ciao."

"Sure, have fun." I smile. I love the fact she has started using 'ciao'. She's sweet, and I hope she doesn't get her heart broken. Italian men do it all the time.

I put my new dress on. I'm not sure why, except it's a shame to spend so much money and have it hang in my closet. I'll just go walking down the strip and maybe grab a sandwich at my favorite shop. I'll follow up on the jobs tomorrow.

I take care to apply makeup like I've seen Ava do, but I don't use nearly as much. I don't wear mascara to make my lashes appear long and alluring.

However, I take time to outline my lips before applying red lipstick and am pleased with the difference it makes. Then I strap on my low-heeled sandals, grab my tiny purse and phone, and walk to the courtyard.

I'm in my own head and bump into the gorgeous stranger from the other day as I'm zipping my purse shut.

"Oh! I'm so sorry, I wasn't paying attention."

"Ah, I met you a few days ago."

"Yes, I remember. Mister . . ." I pause as I'm terrible at names and he caught me completely by surprise.

"Micheli, but you can call me Dante."

"Dante." I let his name roll off my lips like it's melted gelato. Of course, he would have a sexy name to go with his smoking physique and smoldering eyes.

"Juliet, Juliet Accordi." I extend my hand as it seems appropriate.

"Yes, I remember. How could I forget?" He takes my hand in his slender one, and I notice he has a tan and his hands are soft.

His touch stirs my body in places I'm dying to have itched. Now, they've suddenly let their presence be known.

"I was just stopping by to see my friend, but I realize he's probably not here today. I mean, I didn't call ahead. Would you like to grab a coffee?"

"Sure," I say, mesmerized, and I follow him out into the street, where he leads the way.

We walk down a street I've never been on before. It's not very populated. The lizard part of my brain says this street and situation might be dangerous, but my body is telling me to follow this man to the ends of the earth.

"Are we almost there?"

"Yes."

Before I even know what has happened, I find myself with a mesh coffee sack over my head, and I'm being stuffed inside a vehicle. I thrash out in full-blown panic, throwing my hands and legs around, trying to kick anyone and get to freedom until I feel a stab in my arm. My eyes grow heavy. I try to stay awake to figure out where I'm headed as my head slumps against the back of the van's metal wall, but I can't.

* * *

WHEN I COME TO, I have a blinding headache. As my eyes focus, I can see I'm in an amazing wine cellar that looks more like a comfy den than a basement. Even the original cement floor is nicely tiled. I feel zip ties around my wrists, and my ankles are tied to a wooden chair.

As my consciousness tunes in, I can hear men talking behind me softly, and I listen, shifting a little in the seat to get more comfortable, but they hear me.

"Hello," a man says to me as he lifts water to my lips.

I refuse to take it. It could have drugs in it.

He reads me loud and clear. "Relax, it's only water. I can't have you dehydrated."

"I don't believe you. You already knocked me out once." My throat is dry, and my voice is still groggy.

"Sorry about that," he replies, but his face looks incapable of empathy of any kind.

"My body hurts. How long have I been here like this?"

"A few hours," the man says. He has a graying beard and is calm, and in total control.

I'm not going to be able to talk my way out of this or make friends with my captor.

"My parents will look for me," I venture, even though they have no idea I'm missing.

"Oh, we're counting on that," he sneers as he lifts the paper cup of water to my lips.

Drugs or not, I take a drink because I'm thirsty. "What do you mean?"

The man leaves without another word.

I'm left alone in the cellar. How long have I been here? More importantly, when will I be allowed to move? I try to stay calm. There's no point in screaming, I'm sure I'm deep enough in the basement nobody will hear me, and all it will accomplish is waste my energy and piss off my captors. I notice the dusty bottles of wine, and I can tell this collection is worth a king's...

Ransom. Is that what they're doing with me?

It makes no sense. My parents aren't worth lots of money. We get by, but that's it. They save and work very hard. If these guys want money, they have the wrong girl.

A door behind me opens and I hear the heel of a man's dress shoe ring against the tile, but I don't strain my neck to turn. I remain still, waiting for him to reveal himself. My heart beats faster with every passing minute not knowing what's going to happen.

I hate being out of control. I've planned out my life and there is little room for things that don't belong, like being held captive, and I have to assume Dante is part of it as he made no attempt to rescue me.

Then he appears in front of me.

"What the fuck is wrong with you? Coffee and you kidnap me?"

I want to kick him in the nuts, but my legs are still tied, and I'll only hurt myself.

"Untie me," I demand, staring into simmering hazel eyes that don't flinch.

I refuse to look away under his discerning scrutiny, so I zero my eyes in on his. Even though I'm still tired and my body feels like a sack of potatoes, I refuse to look away first. I've watched lots of American shows about killers and I know to try to make friends with them, and find a way to humanize myself so I'll have a better chance of survival.

"Sorry, can't do that yet. Do you know who your father is?"

"Of course, I do. He lives in Greve, he's the town butcher, why do you ask?"

"He's not your father."

I let out a grim chuckle. "You're a stranger and you think you know who my dad is, and it's not my dad? It doesn't seem like you did your homework."

"Oh, that we did. All we need is a DNA test to prove it. The person you call your dad isn't your father."

He is completely and utterly sincere. In a flash, it leads me to doubt everything I've always known to be true, and I'm confused. Who could possibly be my parents, if not the parents I've known my entire life?

"Did you never wonder why you might be an only child?" He pulls a chair from an antique desk in the corner that's sitting on what I assume is an antique rug, judging by the stitching and colors in it. They don't make rugs like that anymore.

"No. But my wrists are growing numb, and my legs hurt." I complain; however, I have no control over my situation.

"Sorry about that." He pulls the chair close to me and turns it backward, then loosens the zip ties before he turns me around again. He straddles me as he leans in, taking a closer look at my face.

If he means to intimidate me, he has the wrong girl. However, his presence is felt when he moves. It's been hours since I was taken, but his suit is fresh and perfect.

Just like his sexy body and handsome face.

"What do you want? My parents don't have money."

"Not the people who raised you, but the father who sired you. Now, he has a kingdom and more money than you can imagine."

"What the . . . sired? You make me feel like a racehorse. I don't know what you're talking about."

The first man returns and hands him a phone. "Cloned, and it's clean."

Fuck. Just when I need technology the most, it's been wiped clean so I can't be located by GPS. Clearly, this isn't their first kidnapping.

"What is it you're after?" I hope to God this isn't a sex trafficking ring. That would be... I don't even want to think about it.

"We're after your biological father. Did you never wonder why your complexion is different from your parents?"

I squirm in the chair. Of course, it's obvious I don't fit in like most Italian families.

Dante pulls out a family picture with me in it from a month ago and holds it at the top, dangling it in front of my eyes so I can view it.

"How did you get that?"

"We'll get into details later. So you're saying you were never told you were adopted?"

My eyebrows come to peaks. "What?"

"Adopted," he smugly replies, putting the picture back in his breast pocket. He stands up abruptly, flicks the chair back to the desk, whips around to face me, and in three long strides, he's within inches of my face.

Damn if he isn't intimidating, yet I fight the urge to turn away.

He peers into my eyes, reading me, and apparently, he's satisfied. Perhaps I'm imagining it, but I think his tone softens just the tiniest bit as he studies me and contemplates what I know and don't know.

"You really don't know, do you?"

"No idea what you're talking about." I want to headbutt him because he's so close to me, but I'm afraid I'd knock myself out if he's as hard-headed as his attitude. "Now, can you cut me loose and let me go home?"

He nods to the first man, who comes out of the shadows behind me and snips the zip ties. "Nothing foolish or you'll be back in them for days," he warns.

The stranger unties my feet, and Dante helps me stand.

The saying is, be careful what you wish for. Sometimes I've wished I had a more eventful life, but I never imagined this in my wildest dreams.

# CHAPTER 10

## DANTE

*D*amn, she's so beautiful, I almost feel guilty about the snatch. But all's fair in love and war, and this is necessary to stop a war, in my opinion.

We took the blood sample while she slept off the sedative so we can test her DNA. Now, we're waiting on official results before our call to Conti. But I don't need to see the results to know she's his. The fact the adoption was kept a secret, and she has no other siblings makes all the pieces fall into place.

I believe her, and yet I wonder how her parents managed to hide her so well. What is their connection in all of this? Or is it just a random occurrence that a child with such dark ties grew up to be so good, decent…and sassy.

Did her adoptive parents know her heritage when they took her in? Did they know Conti? Or her mother? Or are they in the dark as well?

Juliet doesn't seem to be like her biological father, who wouldn't hesitate to stick a knife in your kidney if you looked at him wrong.

When I help her stand, I feel another twinge of guilt, realizing how tired and weak she is from today's ordeal. The plan is already taking a toll on her, and this is only the beginning. Negotiations haven't even started.

I'm a soldier and don't have time to care about her feelings or physical state as long as she's alive and not bleeding out. But it doesn't stop me from moving her up to my kitchen with Riccardo as her personal guard to make sure she doesn't escape. My mansion is a compound, and no one, other than my guards, Riccardo, and my housekeeper, has a reason to be here.

I will find a way to make this situation work. I always do. I'm the don not just because I'm the eldest son in the family, but because I have the skill set and the fortitude to make the business my life. My brothers can marry, give Mama grandchildren, and live a 'normal' life.

I can't let myself feel love or sympathy—those translate into being vulnerable. It's the one advantage I have over Conti. Finding out about Juliet's existence is going to drive him insane, giving me an advantage. Then, I wait and watch him unravel as he realizes his options are limited.

Riccardo and I help Juliet up the steps and I give her the ground rules: "You try to run, I'll shoot you, or Riccardo will, and even if you get past us, don't fool yourself. This is an old estate and doesn't have neighbors. The grounds are crawling with guards."

We sit Juliet down at the kitchen table and my phone dings. It's Alessia. Dammit. She's a sweet girl and sexy as hell but I can't see her again. I like her too much to waste her time. She's getting older and needs to find a nice husband. Plus, I can tell she's growing too attached to me.

I send a curt text saying I'm too busy to see her and she needs to hang out with better men, men who will treat her better than me. She'll get the message.

How much of that was the truth and how much was because I'm fixated on the young vixen sitting in front of me? The one with dark eyes that dart around the room, no doubt counting the guards, identifying the exits, and probably trying to figure out if she can reach the kitchen knives hanging on the wall.

She wants to escape. I'd be surprised if she didn't try. The fact that she's intent on survival impresses me.

"Escaping is a futile effort," I say, pointing out that I'm on to her.

Ignoring me, she looks around the kitchen, seeming to find comfort in no longer being tied to a chair. She rubs her sore wrist, and for that, I'm sorry. I know how painful it can be.

Riccardo opens the microwave to heat up the baked ziti he picked up earlier. Finding plates and forks, he serves Juliet first before placing ours at the table, and we sit down.

Juliet looks at her plate and pushes it away. "I'm not hungry."

"Eat," I command, taking a seat next to her.

"No." Her eyes challenge me, but I stare her down until she lifts her fork and begins to take small bites.

I start to think this through. Normally, I conduct my office work downtown, where the headquarters for the Micheli family business are located. Unfortunately, I don't want to leave Juliet, so I make do on old encrypted computers and burner phones to keep the business going. I don't know how long this will take, and I might not be able to show up at the office tomorrow.

We normally say we're in construction as it covers many things including a sister company that does renovations and other holding companies that make up one parent corporation. Our construction business is not just a simple front because we actually do legitimate work in the industry. But it accounts for little profit, and most of it is from underbidding our competition.

The amount of money we launder through dry cleaners and other small businesses adds up to massive amounts of funds, but because they are small businesses, we avoid unwanted attention. I have also been able to set up some other legitimate restaurants and nightclubs where it is easy to launder money and move products at the same time, mainly drugs. Hotel chains are profitable and another avenue to move drugs in the clubs we have housed in them.

Maybe I can extort money out of Conti, rub it in a little, and let him buy his daughter. But I don't want to always be looking over my shoulder. How can I be certain she is of value to him? The man I met seems to be lacking the fatherly instincts to protect a child unless that child *is* necessary for the official word on Juliet's mother. I suspect Juliet was a love child, from which affair I'm still waiting to hear, and the mother was forced to give her up when Conti's wife got jealous—or maybe Conti's wife never knew, and he wanted to keep it that way. I'm sure I will find out in due course.

It's hard to keep a secret buried for twenty years. And the most unstable element in the mix is Conti himself. I'm not so sure if he can love anyone but himself.

I hope he agrees to strike the bargain we need. He would do well to do business with me because if we are quasi-partners, it will make it more difficult for someone else to strong-arm their way into his business. I don't want his business; I just want to run mine alongside his. I need to make him see I'm the lesser of two evils.

I put food on my fork and try to eat, but having others at the table is strange.

"How long are you keeping me?" Her dark, doe-like eyes implore me.

"Don't know yet."

"Who is my father?"

"It's not safe to tell you that right now." I pick up the glass of red wine Riccardo poured for me as I push back in my seat.

I lift it to my lips and take a much-needed gulp, not a sip. "Do you want some?"

"Sure," she responds, her answer surprising me.

I assumed she'd want to keep her sharp wits about her, but maybe she realizes she's better off playing nice with me. She's young, I'm sure she has a lot to live for and all that.

Riccardo's phone rings, and he takes it outside on the balcony.

"What happens at school when I'm missing?" Juliet looks at me, and I set my wine glass down. I need another refill.

"We came up with a reason for you to go home and left a message. Your roommate is busy with her new boyfriend and thinks you are at your parents', visiting a sick grandmother anyway, so she won't be looking."

Juliet is pensive and takes another small bite before pushing her plate away.

"Bathroom?"

I nod to one of my guards, Flavio, to take her.

Juliet stands and follows him out of the kitchen. There's no way she's getting out of the tiny bathroom window. She's way too short to reach it, and it comes out onto a balcony. Not a slick move on her part, should she try to use it.

I watch her hips sway under the thin minidress as she walks away. The windows are open, letting in the cool night air, so I send a guard to my room to find a light sweater for her to wear.

Tonight will be interesting. Good thing there will be a guard outside her bedroom. I can't sit a foot away from her without my cock straining against my linen pants. It's so hard, one would think it was a flag in a stiff wind. No doubt I'll have blue balls later.

I throw out the question that's been turning in my mind to Riccardo. "Do we call Conti? I think we need to send him pictures. You can tell she looks similar to his sons. They all have the same dark hair and complexion. I bet her mother is Sicilian."

"Maybe. And that makes sense. Lots of times they marry into rival families to keep the peace." Riccardo downs his wine and refills both our glasses.

"I thought of that too, and it's not as outdated a practice as you'd think. I have two brothers who are both eligible bachelors."

"Well, that's convenient." He laughs, and he can't help but smile.

"Yes, it is," I state while reaching into my pants to adjust my throbbing cock.

"You're a sorry sight. She's hot, I can see the effect she has on you."

"Shut the fuck up, Riccardo. No woman has anything on me. I

use them and leave them. She'd be no different, but she deserves to be kept well and treated well because she's worth more that way."

Riccardo takes another gulp of wine. "That we can agree on."

I nod. I'm glad he sees it my way.

I'm beginning to wonder what's taking Juliet so long in the bathroom and ask Flavio to check on her.

I hear him tapping on the door, and she responds, although I can't make out the words. He gives me the thumbs-up; everything is fine.

"Just tell me what you need, Dante." Riccardo is the only one who calls me by my Christian name. It depends on his mood and who's with us.

"What do you need at your end?" I need to know his logistics.

"DNA results tomorrow. And we also need to take some pictures of Juliet to send."

"Do you have the birth certificate?"

"Of course, it's the first official document I copied."

I reach for my wine glass and look toward the bathroom hallway waiting for our guest of honor to return. I didn't peg her as one of those high-maintenance women who spend fifteen minutes in the bathroom to piss and wash her face.

"I think we need to arrange for a shopping day for our guest tomorrow," I announce while pushing my chair back and putting my plate in the sink.

"Are you fucking kidding me?"

"Hear me out. One, she's going to be a handful cooped up here, and two, we don't want her to look like a pauper when we send pictures. It might do us all good. I'll go, in case she has any ideas to ruin our plans. And if she meets anyone she knows, I can run interference."

"Well, I don't like it, but you're calling the shots. I'll arrange a detail to go with us."

This is when I suddenly wish I knew where Alessia shopped. Juliet's personality and figure wouldn't be able to pull off the same clothing, but I'd better find out what stores to take her to. I'd hate to fail at impressing her on our first outing.

Impressing her? Do I have a moment where I've succumbed to her charm? I don't have to impress anyone. She's our captive; I'm just trying to make it less traumatic for her.

But deep inside my heart, I know I'm trying to get a foothold on her without it resulting in the mutually assured destruction of both of us. She has to bend to my will. I'm the don for fuck's sake. I make the rules.

# CHAPTER 11

## JULIET

*J*'m so confused about everything. Dante is easy on the eyes, and I want to hate him, but I can't. I haven't even seen his mansion in the daytime, but if it's anything like him, it's spectacular.

I don't know why there is all this mystery. How is it possible I am adopted and didn't know about it? Why didn't my parents tell me? And who are my real parents who didn't want me and gave me away?

I mean, WTF? I have no answers and no freedom. I hate this. All I wanted was a more exciting life—well, I got it, all right. I didn't even need to throw a coin in the Trevi Fountain.

Bending over the beautiful glass basin in the sumptuous wash-room, I run the cold water for a second before splashing it on my face and washing off my makeup. It's been on for hours and I'm tired. My eyes are bloodshot, and I look like I haven't slept in a week.

I feel bad for using the beautifully embroidered hand towels and find it odd for a bachelor—at least I assume he's a bachelor—would bother with such a small detail. Maybe he hired a decorator or asked his mother for help. Although he doesn't look like a man who asks for help, ever.

Being kidnapped is terrifying, but for some reason, having Dante around makes me feel like I'll come out of this alive. I trusted him, and now I don't, but if shit goes down, I want him on my side, that's for sure. And the guy with the beard, the one who rarely speaks and seems to be with Dante all the time, I wouldn't be surprised if he was trained by some secret service agency, like the Mossad or something. Even though he's older, he's in excellent shape, and looks like he can kick some ass.

There's no use in trying to run away. If these guys want me, they'll be able to keep me. And who's to say there aren't others looking for me? The next band of thugs might not be as accommodating.

I'm angry, and I know I should be a pain in Dante's ass, but he has this way of intimidating me. He speaks to me like he doesn't care and yet, when I look in his eyes, I see desire. I'm sure of it. There's a primal connection that makes my pussy feel a need to be massaged by his hard cock. I can tell by the way he carries himself he's not going to disappoint any woman in that department. Ava calls it 'big dick energy'. I didn't know what she was talking about until now.

Just the touch of his hand on mine in the basement...OMG... my stomach was doing flip-flops, and it wasn't for lack of food. I've never felt that way around a man before. Maybe that's why women my age like older men. They have a calm, self-assured energy from having seen more and done more. I'd be intrigued to date a man who's wise and worldly, even though I have little motivation to get back on the dating circuit because of all the games.

I've learned to compensate for my lack of a social life by using art to fill the void. And I'm getting a job. OMG, I forgot. Job! Crap, I left applications everywhere with my phone number and anyone who calls me will go straight to voicemail. I'll never be able to retrieve any messages because my kidnappers threw out or changed the chip, I'm sure.

Crap, crap, and more crap.

The man guarding the bathroom door is massive and doesn't talk, but I can tell he's Italian. He taps on the door again, and I open it to find him handing me a sweater. It must belong to Dante because his cologne makes my nose tingle, and it reminds me of him. Surprised at his thoughtfulness, I put it on and return to the table, where the Secret Service guy and Dante sit drinking wine.

"So, tell me, what is the deal with my birth parents?" I sit as Dante holds the bottle of wine over my glass to see if I want more, and I nod.

He fills my glass and twists the bottle at the end of the pour, so it won't drip. I'm impressed. That's a trick I learned when I was waiting tables. As a precaution, he sets the empty wine bottle out of my reach. Smart man, but with all the muscle around here, I'm not that stupid.

"Am I in danger every time I go out on the streets? I mean, have I lived with this threat of violence around me my entire life?" I can't believe I'm that oblivious, but then again, I have zero experience with organized crime, which is what I'm assuming this is.

"I don't think so. You were hard to find. You're our enemy's best-kept secret. So, as long as those in my circle keep their mouths shut, you're perfectly safe with me. I can't promise what will happen after your dad finds out."

"I still don't understand the point of grabbing me."

"We've tried the proper channels with a meet, and it didn't go well, which was to be expected. No family is going to give up control of something they acquired at great cost and then share it years later. They're like toddlers clinging to their favorite toy. It would be good for business and make peace for both sides if they were somewhat more accommodating, though," he replies as he twists the stem of the wine glass between his fingers.

"Then why aren't they?"

"Pride, arrogance, machismo, and the need to exert their power just because they can."

I grimace, this sounds like a game of chicken and I'm the one being held over the pot of boiling water. Typical men.

"So, what's next?"

"You're the captive, let me worry about the details." The piercing cold look in his eyes tells me to stop talking.

I sip my wine and lean back in the chair. Ouch! With the amount of money he's poured into this place, you'd think he would have more than wood chairs. Maybe he has a penchant for wooden paddles. I mean, really. My butt is falling asleep and soon my legs will be doing the same.

I let the wine coat my tongue and slide down my throat as I'm in no rush to go anywhere. This is when it strikes me just how lame an existence I've been living. It's pathetic to think all it took was a simple note left for Ava and a message to the dean to explain my absence and no one will miss me.

Even Ava, who just blew in a few weeks ago, has new friends to go places with, social plans, and a good-looking boy toy to fuck. She has a life. What do I have? A hot captor is what I have.

Dante's phone rings. He answers it, listens, then hems and haws before hanging up and putting it in his pocket.

He nods to Mr. Secret Service if I'm to judge by his stance and unemotional face. He's wound tight enough to be part of the Mossad and I wonder what the two of them will talk about when they leave the room. Low voices swirl around the room, but I can't make out the words as the other guards move closer to me. They look stylish in their black polos and matching dress slacks, and I observe their military-style boots.

I glance up at them out of the corner of my eye before staring into my half-empty wine glass. Damn, this wine is good. I get the impression he spares no expense when it comes to things like this. No doubt, he's a man used to getting what he wants.

The two men return to the room and say nothing. The tension

in the room is palpable. I take it something bad happened and they aren't going to discuss it in front of me.

"Did either of you find my original birth certificate, with the names of my birth parents?" I ask, looking for one shred of evidence to prove what they are telling me is true.

"Oh, yes." Dante pulls out his phone and retrieves a file he downloaded. He clicks open and the document springs to life on the screen. I look closely and read the lines for parents. It says my father is D'enotti. There is no name.

"Why does it say of unknown parentage? Shouldn't there be a name there?"

"Yes." Dante closes the phone and places it face down on the table.

"Well, who is it? You do know, don't you?"

He's quiet.

"Who is it? I demand you tell me." As I stand, the guards step closer.

"Not now. It's too dangerous."

"Too dangerous? I've been kidnapped. I find out my parents lied to me and the people who gave me up for adoption wanted to be anonymous. How can this possibly be any more fucked-up or dangerous?"

"Trust me, it is. Flavio will show you to your room. We'll have a guard outside your door tonight and the grounds are covered with them, so you're safe."

What the fuck! Safe? It sounds to me like an overused and misused adjective to patronize me rather than tell me I'm screwed. How can I trust Dante? How can I trust anyone ever again?

I want to go home, but I have less than zero idea where I am, and even if I knew, it would still be difficult. These rural areas don't have buses and I wouldn't be safe getting in a stranger's car. I don't want to risk it.

I'm led up the most gorgeous winding staircase to my room. I look up to find the high ceilings are covered with frescos of angels and demons. It's a sight to behold and reminds me of the Sistine Chapel. I bet most of his goons don't even appreciate all the art and design in this old house.

Judging from the walls that show no nicks in the paint, this place has been redone recently. It must have taken an army of skilled craftsmen to paint the ceiling, lay the stonework for the arched doorways, and install the ornate crown molding and columns in the marble foyer. Dante clearly has money.

My feet are tired as I walk barefoot across the spotless tile floor. Either he has a maid visit every day or he's never home.

At the top of the stairs, I'm shown to a room with a canopy bed so high I'll need a pole vault to get in it. It reminds me of a cloud, all white and covered with pillows for sleeping and three throw pillows for decoration.

The only flash of color in the room is a pale blue shirt at the foot of the bed. It's a man's shirt. I guess I won't have to sleep in my dress after all.

The bed looks too pretty to use, but I'm too wiped out to care as I pull back the fluffy duvet. Tomorrow will be here soon enough, and I'm sure it will bring a whole new set of surprises.

# CHAPTER 12

## JULIET

*D*ante is delicious. For any man to be that sexy, first thing in the morning has to be a cardinal sin to the nth degree. I try to keep from drooling as I set his coffee in front of him, but it's impossible to ignore the fact he's only wearing jeans, and his naked chest is covered in dark hair. I want to run my fingers through his chest hair which is covering nipples I want to tug on.

I'm torn. He's a criminal, and I hate him for turning my life upside down, but at the same time, he took me away from my boring life, and I feel more alive than ever before. I honestly can't decide if I should despise him or if I'm falling in love with him. But I do wonder what he's packing in his jeans. He fills them out so well, I can understand why women throw themselves at him. No doubt they do. If I learned anything from Ava, it's the subliminal cues of the mating process.

Mr. Secret Service says nothing as he hands me some different clothes. According to Dante, I have zero fashion sense. Maybe the red dress really did make me look cheap. I have no clue. I figured if it looked good on Ava, it would look good on me.

For a moment, I wonder how her romance with her boy toy is

going, but then I decide I need to worry more about myself. If I fall for Dante, what will my life be like? Will I be locked away on this estate and disappear from society altogether? I have to surface at some point, don't I?

I look around, enjoying being in the car without a bag on my head this time. The car is state of the art with gadgets I've never seen. The estate is even more impressive than I imagined. The stone edifice manages to be massive and welcoming at the same time. Maybe it's the terracotta pots full of lemon trees and the pink bougainvillea covering the terrace giving it a warm vibe. It's certainly not the master of the house.

We slowly make our way past the rows of cypress trees lining the driveway and down a large hill. The switchbacks are vaguely familiar, but once we merge onto the highway, I recognize nothing.

Seeing a sign indicating an airport ahead, I panic. "What? Where are we going?" I lean forward too quickly in my seat and stop when I feel the seatbelt lock up, cutting into my shoulder. I sense the guard next to me tense.

"You said shopping. Who takes a plane to go shopping? Is this a trick to fly me to a salty grave somewhere?"

It's the first time I hear Dante's deep chuckle.

"Quite the opposite, my little artist. It appears your creativity lies in your artwork. You just need to think of yourself as that blank sheet of paper you sketch for school."

I let out a huff of frustration. He knows everything about me and my life, but I know nothing about him. I'm no Nancy Drew, but I need to figure my way out of this situation before it's too late.

"How do you know what I do?" I challenge him.

"You'd be surprised." The deep timbre of his voice tickles my lady parts, and I feel a dampness between my legs. Why do I find this bad boy so wildly exciting?

Out of the car and happy to stretch my legs, I strut across the tarmac one step behind Dante like I've done this a million times. What is it Ava says? Fake it 'til you make it? Something like that.

I'm not going to be some shrinking violet in his presence. I'm sure he's had his share of women, and I'm not trying to compete with any of them, but with the right tools, maybe I can give him something other than work to think about.

As soon as we boarded the jet and settled in our seats, a flight attendant hands us each a mimosa. This is something I could get used to. Then my eyes catch a few more bodyguards sitting in the twelve-seater jet who look like they went to the same school as Mr. Secret Service. An hour later, the flight attendant collects our empty glasses as we prepare to land. Looking out the window, I see snow-capped mountains in the distance and assume we must have flown north.

Following Dante down the narrow steps of the plane, I ask, "Where are we?"

"Hmm, I'm surprised you don't know. I'll give you a clue," he jests, "The Last Supper is here."

I keep up with his long strides across the tarmac and think quickly. "Oh, you mean Milan?"

"Very good, Juliet," he replies with a smile.

I love how my name rolls off his tongue and wonder what it would sound like if he moaned it instead.

So, this is Milan, the capital of fashion and design and home of the famous The Last Supper by Leonardo da Vinci, located in the Santa Maria delle Grazie church. I couldn't call myself an art student if I didn't know this. It's exciting to be here in person. Leo is one of my favorite artists, and Mom and I always watch the annual runway fashion shows on television, but I wish this trip was under slightly different circumstances.

I follow Dante as we climb into a large black SUV waiting for us outside the airport. This time, Dante is in the back seat with me, and it crosses my mind to make a break for it, but where would I go?

Part of me is intrigued by this mysterious man sitting next to me. I catch a whiff of citrus and salt with a manly hint of leather coming off him when the air-conditioning vent blows it past my nose. It's like a breeze off the Mediterranean. I wonder at his intent. He sat in the front seat on the way to the airport this morning. Why switch it up now?

I know he thinks ahead, and I wouldn't be surprised to find out he's a master at manipulation. Meanwhile, the aroma is delicious enough to cause a tingling sensation in my crotch. In my nervousness, I squirm in my seat and my thigh rubs against his.

I can only imagine he's been watching and following me for some time. To know where I live, to show up at my university... judging from the new panties I received this morning, he even knows what kind of underwear I like. I find it unnerving, and yet flattering he's taken the time to think of all these details, even if his hired goons actually carried out the tasks.

"You okay?" he asks with a smirk.

Damn him, he knows what he does to women. He's enjoying this. I find it disturbing and yet thrilling.

This is crazy. I'm playing a cat-and-mouse game with a man who's probably killed people. He already knows everything about me and my family, and my mom and dad are not my biological parents. How could they hide that from me for so long? They must have a good explanation for doing what they did, and one day soon, I'll find out.

"Um, just fine." I refuse for one minute to let him know I find him attractive, even though it is probably becoming painfully obvious.

The car stops and Mr. Secret Service jumps out to open my door. Dante is at my side as we cross the cobblestone street and slips my arm through his. Normally, I would swoon at his gallantry, but I'm sure it's more a calculated move to prevent me from fleeing. Not sure why he's worried about that. We're being followed closely by two armed guards the size of gladiators, so what would be the point?

We arrive at an enormous mall with more shops than I could have imagined, displaying names like Versace, Gucci, and Louis Vuitton. Oh, how I'd love to have one of those handbags. I've never been able to afford a wallet, let alone a purse, but I've loved the designers since I was a kid.

The vaulted ceiling is made entirely of glass, and the floor is covered in marble mosaic. We stroll past beautiful women dressed like models, and I suddenly feel underdressed, even though I'm wearing a nice pair of jeans.

I still have on my wedges and I'm happy to have Dante's arm to guide me because I'm not paying attention to where I'm walking. I'm too busy looking at four stories of shops, bars, and cafés. My artistic eye can't get enough of the sculptures and frescoes. I wish I had my phone to take pictures of all this.

Dante leads me into one shop after another. I finally work up the nerve to peek at a price tag and it's over one thousand euros for a pair of pants. My head swims with the scent of his cologne when he leans close enough to kiss me and murmurs in my ear, "We're spending lots of money today, get used to it."

I don't know which makes me more nervous—how much money he's willing to spend on me, or his close proximity. He not only smells good, but he also looks good in his tailored Armani suit. We've been walking in the heat for a while and I'm starting to perspire, but he still looks just-out-of-the-shower fresh. How does he do it?

The assistants in the shops are diligent in their efforts to bring me countless outfits to try on while I pop in and out for Dante's approval. They bring different sizes, colors, you name it, it's like a scene out of Pretty Woman except we're in Milan. I can't deny I'm having a blast, but I'm also not naïve. I know there will be a reckoning for this, and he will want something from me in return.

By the time I have accumulated four large bags of shoes and dresses, the place is swarming with people, like ants at a picnic.

Looking at the goons carrying all our purchases makes me want to laugh. I should be concerned about the guards holding me hostage, but I'm having fun for the first time in my life.

"Can we please eat? I need water, food, and maybe more caffeine."

No sooner do I ask, than a maître d' greets us at the door of what looks to be the fanciest café in the whole place. Peeking inside, I see linen-covered tables and Murano glass chandeliers casting a warm inviting glow throughout the dining area.

The maître d' asks if we'd like to sit inside or outside.

"Your choice," Dante says.

I'm happy he has given me control over something so trivial. I reply, "Outside," making the decision just the same.

Dante requests bottled mineral water, both sparkling and still. Two waiters attend to us even though the café is crowded. Somehow, I get the feeling there would be a table for us even if the place were filled to capacity.

"Wine?"

"Sure."

He orders a bottle of Pinot Grigio, and it arrives along with a bucket of ice. I feel a little conspicuous at all the attention as baskets of bread and plates of olive oil arrive.

A plate of antipasto shows up with different cured meats, cheeses, and olives to nibble on. I'm famished and want to eat everything in sight, but I know more is coming and hold back. This is Italy; there's always more food.

My dish of veal Milanese does not disappoint. I would have licked my plate if I didn't have an audience. Dante watches my every move between bites of his frutti di mare and seems to approve of my healthy appetite. Dante's right-hand man, Mr. Secret Service, ate risotto and ossobuco and still had room for tiramisu. These boys can eat.

When in Rome, eat like a Roman. We're in Milan, so I'm

enjoying the northern cuisine which is so different from my own. Normally, I would order calamari in a red sauce, but there is nothing normal about today or yesterday.

I trust whatever Dante has been stewing over will be over soon. I'd like to see his sexy fucking smile again . . . among other things.

# CHAPTER 13

## DANTE

*I* try my best to hide my amusement at Juliet's first real experience with designer fashion in every shop. I can't help cracking a smile as I catch a glimpse of her glowing face while she tries on a Prada belt. The sparkle in her eyes outshines the bling on the buckle.

Not to mention the kick I get out of watching her try on sky-high Christian Louboutin heels for the first time. Like a baby deer on unsteady legs, she holds onto the sofa while I pretend not to notice her ankles wobbling. The salesgirl holds her hand and shows her how to keep her shoulders over her hips. After several minutes, I feel confident she can wear them without falling headfirst into a punch bowl.

We continue walking through the galleria now packed with tourists, many of them wealthy like me, with more money than we know what to do with, who don't bother looking at price tags and never ask what something costs.

I notice many of the young women are with older men. I have no doubt many of them are bought and paid for with some unspoken arrangement I call the marriage bargain. The young wife gets the lavish lifestyle, and the old husband gets the arm candy and the price tag that comes with it. As much as I'm a self-made man with a taste for vengeance, I still hope to have more to look forward to in my old age, if I'm lucky to live that long.

I'd rather die than have to buy a woman to be with me, but then, if I'm not going to have kids or marry, I'm destined to be old and alone—if I should outlive my father, that is, and all of a sudden, it's real to me. The life of solitude I vowed to keep doesn't look as good as it sounded.

I give Juliet some space while she picks out intimate wear, but tell the sales associate I want everything in the collection, not just the practical pieces. She gives me a knowing grin and says she'll take care of it, and I'll be very happy.

Flavio pays the cashier as Juliet drops a tiny vibrator from the counter into her purse, and I have to stifle my amusement. She surprises me with her boldness. Was it for fun, or is she horny?

"Oh, these are so cute!" Juliet interrupts my salacious thoughts of what I could do that would satisfy her more than the vibrator, but I proceed without a comment as we leave the lingerie store. It appears she might be stepping out of her shell and dabbling into morally gray areas.

She dashes into a shoe store to get a closer look at a pair of denim Vieira P Strass Orlato sneakers she spotted in the window. She's got a good eye; they will look perfect with those tight jeans she's wearing, the ones hugging her perfect ass. She lets out a squeal of delight when the saleswoman finds them in her size.

I stifle a chuckle at her youthful energy. I have to remind myself she's younger than me and the tie-dye look is her style, not mine.

Riccardo scoffs at her youthful glee, but I have to admit I'm enjoying today, being able to relax and take the moments as they come, moments that aren't covered in blood and filled with family drama.

It's a refreshing and welcome break from what I encounter on a daily basis. I cherish the moment before I nod and say, "We'll take them."

At this point, there is not a chance in hell I'm not sleeping with her. She deserves better than me, but we all have our crosses to bear in life. If Conti doesn't like it, then it might mean war, and it's probably inevitable anyway.

My phone vibrates. Conti? I walk outside, putting on my Polaroid sunglasses as the late afternoon sun is still intense. Riccardo follows me, giving Flavio a signal to stay with Juliet.

"Pronto," I answer the phone, and Conti's labored breathing is at the other end.

"You are truly the scum of the earth, Dante. I'm surprised your mother didn't suffocate you in your sleep when you were small. You better not hurt her."

"I can assure you, Conti, she is fine. But I want what I want—the same agreement you had with my father, without a drop of blood spilled, or she won't be fine anymore."

"How do I know I can trust you? Your father double-crossed me and stole shipments that were mine."

"Listen to me, Conti. We have a new situation. I'll guarantee your daughter's safety by keeping your secret, if you abide by our agreement."

"You ask too much of an old man," he fumes, his anger exploding like Mount Etna as his voice booms through the receiver so loud, I have to hold it away from my ear. I hope he has a strong heart. Otherwise, he might not make it through this phone call.

"How did you find her, anyway?" His gruff undertone gives way to what could almost be interpreted as fondness for a child he has never met.

"It's not important," I reply dismissively, refusing to play along. He might be tracing the call, and I need to keep this short.

"I want to see her. Send me a picture as proof of life." There is a pause, then he asks, "Does she know about me?"

"She knows the people who raised her aren't her biological parents, but I didn't tell her about you. Why tell her when you have so many enemies? Why break her heart?"

He makes a groaning sound. I can't tell if it's regret over her or the fact that my words hit home.

"For that small favor, I thank you, but don't take this as a sign of weakness. The score is not even by any means. I can put a hit out on her just as easily as I can on you," his raspy voice comes across as the threat it's meant to be.

"Ciao." I hang up. It's a way to retain power as I control the pace, the time, the meet. I can tell he still thinks I'm too young to be the head of the Micheli family, but I ran the streets as a kid before I went away to school. Just because I was in England getting an MBA from Oxford doesn't mean my street crew and my family were ever far from my thoughts.

Who does he think designed the skimmers that scan the credit card numbers of unsuspecting tourists as they walk around thinking their wallets are safe in their ridiculous fanny packs? At Oxford, I made international contacts, and those contacts have paid off. I also learned money breeds influence, and that more money means more influence.

"She's his," I tell Riccardo matter-of-factly.

"Fuck, that's brilliant," he says with a grin as he takes a long drag on his vape pen.

I leave him to watch the door as I go back into the store to pay the cashier. The four of us hit the streets, and I'm ready for a hotel. This shopping shit is exhausting. I don't know how women have the energy for it.

But first, I hand my phone to Riccardo, instructing him to take a picture of me and Juliet. Even though we are still nowhere near a resolution with her father, I made progress today, and it justifies a celebration.

"Come, let's check into the hotel and get some rest before dinner." I quickly add, "The shops will be closing soon." Juliet's face falls in disappointment; one would think I just took away her new Jimmy Choos.

"One tiny gelato?" she pleads, looking at me ever so sweetly, batting her lashes as she makes fun of herself for pulling out all the stops to influence me and knowing she's not the type to do such a thing. She must really want this gelato, as her eyes implore me to indulge her in one last treat today. Even though I'm a monster with everyone but my family and Riccardo, I acquiesce.

"One. Then we must go." We walk toward the gelateria.

This woman loves her gelato, and she asks the shopkeeper for two scoops, one lemon, and one raspberry. This combination seems disgusting to me, mixing both tart and sweet flavors, but she appears thrilled.

She carefully uses the tiny spoon to scoop a bit of each flavor and offers me a taste. With her arm extended toward me, I notice her skin is a shade darker than this morning and realize she's getting a tan from the time we've been outside.

"I'll throw up if I eat that," I protest as I turn my face away from her.

"You'll love it, trust me, it will change your world," she coaxes me.

I can't refuse her charm and sense of adventure, something I lost years ago. For once, I choose to live vicariously through her.

"Okay, one." I bend my head toward her hand, close enough to breathe her in, welcoming her clean scent like a cool breeze after a summer rain. I wonder what her lips taste like, and I want to know what it feels like to lick between her legs and give her the most incredible orgasm of her life.

The gelato is cold, but not cold enough to keep my cock from filling out my dress pants. I need a cold shower before I take her in the next available dressing room and give her a taste of what I've got, but the carnal idea is so appealing.

She slides the spoon into my mouth and holds it steady. I take the gelato into my hot mouth, and we exchange lustfully dangerous looks before we both retreat, like shy teenagers.

She offers me another taste, and again the thrill of being so intimate with her, as if we've lovers, makes me wrap my lips around the tiny spoon and our eyes lock. Hers flicker with sexual attraction before darting away, denying me the satisfaction of knowing if she's lusting for me too.

"Hate to break this up, but we need to move," Riccardo says as our Rolls Royce Cullinan pulls up with Flavio behind the wheel. The purchases are loaded into the back, and I sit next to Juliet, moving closer to make sure she's not trying to lull me into a false sense of security.

I curse her jeans for covering up her sexy legs, and I would lean in closer if not for the damn seatbelt. Good thing it's only a short ride to our five-star hotel because it's the only thing keeping my cock from going off.

Flavio drops us off at the marble and glass entrance, and the bellman takes our purchases and all our overnight bags.

Juliet, clearly in awe of the plush reception area, has all the wonder of a child in an adult body. The lobby is quieter than normal. I take hold of her elbow, guiding her away from the check-in desk and heading straight to a private elevator.

"Where are we going? Am I meeting my father?"

"No."

She wants more information, but this isn't the place.

"When? I want to meet him."

"Hush, or I'll have to punish you," I whisper. I can't have her making demands of me in front of my men. Plus, I haven't figured out how Conti will twist this to his advantage. No doubt he's working on a plan to either get her back or kill me for double-crossing him, or both.

"I have to run out briefly while you rest."

"Are you leaving me with the guards again?"

"They have names, Flavio and Riccardo. I suggest you use them, otherwise, it's just rude. I won't tolerate insolence from anyone, especially you."

I'm tired of playing babysitter. Work is calling. I have contacts to meet, and I'm taking Riccardo with me. He's almost always with me. The only exception is when I sneak off and no one knows where I am, like to get an espresso.

Juliet walks beside me as we pass hotel staff on our way to the back of the building and enter the private elevator, where Riccardo uses a card key in the elevator to make it move and hits the button P. She remains quiet for the short ride up to the penthouse.

After the elevator stops, Flavio pulls out the key card, and I put my arm out to stop Juliet from getting out.

"Please, Ms. Accordi, wait here until I give you an all-clear," Flavio says as he walks into a magnificent penthouse that is more of a home away from home.

From Juliet's gasp, I'm sure she expected just a hotel room, but she should know by now I'm not an average man.

# CHAPTER 14

JULIET

*J*'m tense until Dante moves behind me and puts a hand on my arm as if he's protecting me from some imaginary foe. Or is he just looking for an excuse to touch me?

His hand is warm and surprisingly soft, sending a shiver of excitement up my spine. The level of sexual tension between us is off the charts, and I'm exhausted from the overwhelming day of shopping. The fact that we can never let our guard down, even when we're traveling, is a clear indication more is going on than he's sharing with me. Maybe he's right; I need to lie down and rest. Can I lie down with him?

Flavio returns. "All clear, boss."

Dante nods and his hand falls away from my arm. "You may move around as you like."

I fling him a look and saunter over to the windows to check out the scenery. The windows run from floor to ceiling and take up the entire wall. I've never been surrounded by such jaw-dropping opulence, and with no blinds or drapes, the view does not disappoint. Outside is a rooftop garden decorated with sculptures and fountains, shaded by a pergola covered with climbing roses blooming in every color.

As beautiful as it is, I feel exposed and cross my arms protectively, as I would if I were cold. Dante takes his jacket off, puts it around my shoulders, then leaves without a word.

What was that about? He's giving me a lot of mixed signals and I'm not sure what to make of it. I wonder what he has planned for me. For us. Am I sharing a room with him?

He won't tell me anything and I know better than to ask his goons. No way are they doing anything to piss him off.

I don't know how they can enjoy spending their lives waiting for him to tell them what to do, but it's probably all they've ever known. Maybe my parents gave me up so I didn't have to live this restrictive lifestyle.

I continue my exploration of the suite, walking through the dining area, tracing my finger along a mahogany table set for dinner for eight. Two beautiful chandeliers hang from the vaulted ceiling, one at each end of the table. I pick up a piece of china and turn it over. Of course, it's Limoges. I roll my eyes and put it back, carefully. I don't even bother to check the water glasses. They're probably Waterford crystal.

The living room has a black leather sectional that takes up most of the room, and the biggest television I've ever seen. Someone in the next building could watch that TV without needing binoculars.

I glance into the full kitchen with its beautiful stone countertops, the latest stainless-steel appliances, and a backsplash made entirely of sea glass. I love to collect sea glass and make a mental note to do the same in my own kitchen someday. The fixtures and faucets look like shiny ornaments that have never been used.

"Ah, good to be home," Riccardo sighs, making his way through the kitchen on his way to his room, I presume.

Flavio is still standing guard by the exit when Dante appears out of nowhere. If this is a mob hideout, I wouldn't be surprised if the place has trapdoors and secret passages.

"My room?" My eyes beseech his.

"Yours is over there, on the left. And don't try anything to make me regret bringing you," he threatens.

I wonder if he could ever be in a relationship where he's not barking orders.

Heading in the direction he pointed, I stroll to my room and find all my packages inside, along with some art supplies I didn't even know he bought. The room is straight out of a movie, only even more grandiose, with heavy dark blue drapes over the windows; again, they extend from the floor to the ceiling. I can make out afternoon shadows on the building across the way, an office building perhaps.

I've never been in a penthouse suite, but now I can understand the attraction and could easily get used to this. I just wonder what price Dante has in store for me since he's lavishing me with privileges I've never known.

The windows are closed and we're so high up, I can barely hear the horns and sirens from the traffic below. In this rarefied air, I can almost forget I'm being held against my will. With Flavio guarding the door, the only way out of this place is to jump, or to be rescued by Spider-Man.

I start to look through my haul of designer things, wondering if we will be going out to dinner, and if so, where we will go and what I should wear.

I find Dante intriguing, even though he is cold and aloof. His standoffish demeanor doesn't give me much of an opportunity to get to know who he is. I mean, was he born a cold-blooded killer, or did he grow into the role and the life? I'd like to ask him about that.

Either way, I decide there is no way I could ever take him home to meet my parents, knowing who he is and guessing what he must do for a living.

My feet are sore from walking all day, and I kick off my wedges thankfully. I pick up a pretty notepad on the nightstand, stenciled with the same blue color as the curtains. The name of the hotel is at the bottom, and in fine print under it, it reads, 'Micheli Enterprises'. Holy shit, he must own this hotel. That would explain the private elevator and the penthouse.

I wonder how many other properties he owns. For now, I'm content to find one more piece of the puzzle that is Dante Micheli. I figured it out on my own without having to ask questions, questions that only seem to piss him off.

I'm feeling a bit smug and pleased with myself as I curl into a ball on the bed. And with only the low murmur of voices in the other room, I soon slip into a nap.

A finger brushes across my forehead and it wakes me. Blinking, I look up into the sexiest pair of eyes watching me. Dante is standing over me, and the intensity of his gaze gives me a fit of nervousness as he passes by.

"Follow me." He holds out his hand.

I don't hesitate to put my hand in his. I have no idea what he wants, but I have a feeling it's time to pay the price for this luxurious penthouse.

# CHAPTER 15

## DANTE

*I*t's nice to be back here at the penthouse. I haven't been up this way in quite some time. There's not much I can do about the Albanians gaining in strength and numbers, but we still have some territory and connections up here, so it doesn't hurt to show my face and pay some people a visit to say hello.

For instance, we have a meeting lined up with the mayor, which we head to. He's got a gambling problem, and we carry his vig for him. I also contribute to his campaign fund, and in exchange, he uses his political connections to give me influence where my money wouldn't otherwise be welcome.

I checked on Juliet before Riccardo, and then I left to meet with the mayor of Milan. It turns out his campaign for re-election needs an infusion of cash after all. I am more than happy to oblige. One never knows when having a direct line to someone who owes me will prove to be useful.

Riccardo and I return to the penthouse and step out onto the garden terrace so we can have a conversation without having to worry about Juliet overhearing us while she explores my home away from home. I take a minute to take in the evening stars, plentiful on such a clear night. Deep in thought, I rub my hand across my jaw, as I always do, and I curse myself once again for starting this pissing match with Conti and especially for dragging Juliet into it.

She preoccupies my mind, even during my darkest moments. She's a good person and lives a normal life. Now I've messed that up for her. I brought her into this life, the life her mother sacrificed everything to keep her away from. I didn't realize how this will affect her after she's of no use to me. But it's clear she'll probably never be safe as long as Conti breathes. He's a man stuck in the past, hell-bent on vengeance.

"Yeah, he threatened us, so we have to increase security," I break my silence at last. "I don't know which one of us he wants to get rid of, maybe both." Riccardo opens a bottle of Dewar's and pours a glass for each of us.

"Drink," he grumbles, sounding more like Russian KGB than Italian.

I chuckle, he's a stand-up guy and I'm glad he has my back twenty-four/seven. He values my life as much as he values his own, maybe more. He never married and has no children to carry on the family name. His only sister followed her husband to Switzerland, and his mother lives in a small condo in Florence. He pays her bills and stops by when he can. He's a good son and a loyal employee.

After brushing a few stray leaves off a cushioned chair, I drag it to a bistro table and sit. Riccardo joins me and pulls two cigars from his jacket, clips the ends, and hands me one along with a lighter. I light up and hand the lighter back. We lean back in our chairs and enjoy our brief moment of peace and solitude.

I blow out a ring of smoke and watch the circles rise until a light breeze carries them away. "We need to plan for Conti to act as crazy as he usually does. A leopard doesn't change its spots. Not even for Juliet," I muse.

"On it, boss. I think a church meeting would be best, it's the safest. We just need to find one with security and be extra careful getting in and out," Riccardo suggests.

Quietly, I take another puff on my cigar. I like his plan and was thinking the same thing myself.

"There's a million churches in Florence, but only one with security like that, and the line is so long, we'd never get in."

"What about Siena? It's a bit of a drive, but it's our territory and I have a contact who can get us in if lines are an issue," Riccardo offers.

"I like that. Yes, that could work." I lean back and gaze at the clear sky, but in truth, all I can think about is Juliet. From the day we met in the courtyard, I have found her intriguing and can't get enough of her. I could stare at her all day.

She seems shy, almost timid, but she handles herself with poise for someone completely outside their comfort zone. She catches on quickly. Smart girl, I grin.

I'm not sure how she's going to handle meeting Conti. I imagine he'll turn on the charm and spew lies, and she will believe him because we never want to think anyone, especially our parents, can lie to us.

I'm prepared for her to be sucked in by him in the beginning, but it won't be long before the facade cracks and she will see him for who he truly is. Then she probably won't want anything to do with him. So why meet at all?

Now, I'm thinking it's best if they never meet. He will always be watching her, and I don't want her living the rest of her life worried that he could take her at any time and that I might not be there to prevent it. I started this and it's my duty to keep her safe. Who am I kidding? She'll never be safe as long as he lives, and I'm not safe either. The only way we can be free is if he's dead, but I can't kill another don. That would bring another bloodbath and garner the attention of the authorities from every office in Italy, and we want to avoid that at all costs. It hurts business.

Conti is so powerful, he even has ambulances turn their sirens off in neighborhoods in the south because it interferes with selling drugs on the streets. Customers think the police are coming, as their sirens sound alike, so he leaned on a few people and presto, like magic, the sirens don't blare in the suburbs. That's some kind of muscle.

"Conti will always be a problem, always has been, always will be," Riccardo observes as he exhales a puff of smoke from the Cuban cigar. "I'm surprised he hasn't made more trouble for you over the years, to be honest."

I murmur an absent agreement to Riccardo's observation, but in truth, my mind is consumed by imagining what Juliet would look like in her new lingerie. I know she's just inside the penthouse and my cock grows hard with just the knowledge that she's so close.

I take a swig of the Dewar's. It cools the warm cigar smoke in my throat and chest. Guy time is great, but there's a pussy inside I own, and I can't push my cock's needs off any longer. I down my scotch in one swallow and stand. "I'm taking a short break," I say gruffly, and I leave Riccardo and enter the quiet penthouse.

I make my way to Juliet's room and find her napping. She looks so peaceful as I push the hair away from her angelic face. When her eyes open, she doesn't look surprised to see me. In fact, she smiles a sleepy smile and stretches.

"Follow me," I murmur quietly. I extend my hand and feel a ping of joy she's not fighting me when she accepts it. In the end, it doesn't matter if she wants me or not, because she's mine and I won't let her go, not to Conti and certainly not to an arranged marriage to one of my brothers. That is now totally out of the question.

She notices the hard cock in my trousers and as she stands, she looks up and our eyes meet. There's a fire in her eyes, and it's for me.

I lead her to my room, tastefully decorated, not overly fancy or cluttered. The bed is huge by European standards. Most of the bedrooms here aren't large enough for king-size beds, but this one is.

As soon as I close the door behind us and slip out of my jacket, I grab her by the back of her neck and pull her toward me. My lips and tongue unleash a powerful assault on her soft mouth. It takes a second for her to respond to my demands, and when she does, her lips ferociously attack mine. I pull back, take a breath, and give her a wry smile.

"You like this," she says, taunting me.

"Shut up and fuck me hard," I growl. I like it a bit rough, but I'll have to break her in gently.

Her fingers work at my buttons as I remove her clothing and we let it all drop to the floor. I want to enjoy all of her as I strip her of her bra and panties.

She lies back on the bed, and I crawl toward her, more like she's my prey than a lover. I explore her entire body with my mouth until she reaches up and grabs my hair, pulling me down to her pussy.

I inhale her scent as I run my tongue down her abdomen, then lick up her inner thighs, one leg first, then the other, and she squirms under me.

"Do not move," I command.

She obeys and lies still as my tongue hits her soft lips and flicks over her clit, but she pulls on my hair, which makes me even harder. I want to be inside her but am still resolved to take it slow. Postponing the excitement will make the final orgasm more intense. To make this a quickie would be depriving us both.

I play with her, drinking in her nectar and sucking her nub as if I need it to sustain life. She tastes so sweet. I dip two fingers in, rubbing her G-spot and making her arch her back off the bed before I pull them out and lick them as I look deep into her eyes.

She seems surprised by this and moans as her hands fall off my shoulders and clutch the bedspread. "Now... fuck me now, I can't take it anymore," she pants.

My cock thickens even more than I thought humanly possible. I'm more than happy to accommodate the lady's request. I lean over her and position my cock at the entrance to her pussy. "Is this what you want, Princess?"

"Yes." Her moan is but a whisper and I can tell she's ready to pop.

"You have to promise not to come right away."

"Ahhh..." She moans in frustration, but I'm loving the fact that I can drive her crazy.

"Promise," I command.

"Okay, fuck you," she spits at me for being the prick I am, but I chuckle and lean over her as I enter her and hear her cry with pleasure.

I move slowly to calm her throbbing pussy as her muscles tighten around my thick cock and her hips move with mine. Her nails rake down my back, and when I'm satisfied I've made her wait long enough, she comes hard, crying out so loud the people in the next building probably heard.

I wait until her orgasm recedes before slowly thrusting into her wetness. As I feel the pressure building up, I resist the urge to come, waiting for it to build to a crescendo of pleasure that overtakes me. Suddenly, my cock explodes in ecstasy and a loud moan escapes my lips like never before.

I collapse and lie next to her, sharing the afterglow. She cuddles up next to me, and I let her. I'm not looking for cuddles or tenderness, but in this moment, nothing else exists but the two of us in this bubble, and it feels nice for a change.

I roll away from her and sit on the edge of the bed. She rubs her soft hand over the center of my back.

"Nice tattoo. The Archangel Michael?"

"Yes, protector over evil. I'm evil, but I still need protecting," I murmur as I stand up to head to the shower built for two. "Come. We need to get cleaned up and find something to eat."

# CHAPTER 16

## JULIET

*a*fter leaving Dante's room, I head to the one he's assigned me to clean myself. He mentioned food, but I don't know what time it is. Without a watch or phone, it's hard to tell. I can only go by the soft glow of what looks to be early evening stars outside my window. I look in the antique mirror over the dresser, run a comb through my straight black hair, and decide I need some makeup. Dante insisted on the best, of course. I dust some bronzing powder onto my face and apply red lipstick with a touch of gloss to make them look moist.

There. That's as good as it's going to get for the moment until I know where we're going for dinner. Now, I prepare myself to be scrutinized by the men as I make my way to the living room, curious as to what I may have missed since leaving Dante's room.

It's getting dark outside, and Italians in the north tend to eat dinner a bit earlier than Tuscans. Flavio is sitting in the kitchen with an espresso and greets me while reaching into his pocket to pull out my phone.

"Your mother called. You may call her back now, but no tip-offs on anything," he warns, "otherwise, there will be consequences."

"Okay." I snap the phone out of his hand and tentatively read the text message. I ring my mother, afraid I might say the wrong thing but welcome the opportunity to hear a familiar voice.

"Ava and I are fine, Mama," I reassure her after she picks up on the first ring and chastises me for taking so long to call her back. After she gets me caught up on her week, I tell her I love her and ask her to give Dad a hug for me. I manage to hang up without mentioning the fact she's not my real mother.

Dante and Riccardo come in from the elevator, and I have to wonder where they went for the twenty minutes I took getting cleaned up. Judging from their relaxed demeanor, whatever they were up to went well. I think it's the first time I've seen either of them look close to happy.

"Great." Dante rubs his hands together gleefully. "Where to for dinner? I want loads of seafood."

"Good," Riccardo agrees before slipping out on the balcony to vape.

"What should I wear?" I ask Dante.

"That cute little number that shows off your legs. I think it was a pastel blue."

"All right," I agree. Everything is so beautiful, I don't care what I wear it. I just want an opportunity to look chic and grown-up for a change.

I turn on my heel and head back to my room. I still need to get him alone and find out who my father is. My wardrobe may have changed, but my priorities have not.

But right now, I need to figure out what shoes to wear with the pale blue dress now that I've wriggled into it. I want to wear my new heels but don't know if Dante will help me across the tricky sidewalks and cobblestone streets. I decide to chance it and slip on the stilettos before touching up my lips. Dropping the Ferrari red lipstick in my new Fendi handbag, I deem myself ready to go.

I return to the living room just in time to hear Riccardo recommend a restaurant nearby. Flavio agrees it's the best place in town for seafood. Every Italian knows that you only eat seafood near the coast, and we're only three hours away from the Med, so I can't wait.

The energy shifts as soon as Dante walks into the room. All eyes focus on him when he's around. His commanding presence demands it. He's like a singer who's lucky to be born with that elusive star quality that makes everyone want to watch them—fascinating, alluring, and charismatic. It's no wonder I feel like a teenage girl with a crush on her favorite boy band whenever he's near me.

But I'm not a teenager and he's clearly not a member of a boy band. The man has practically grown a beard since he shaved this morning. I like his five o'clock shadow and recall how it felt against my skin. I'm glad he didn't shave it. It goes well with the crisp shirt he's just changed into, another dress shirt that cost more than the last one, judging from the price tags I saw today. But his shirts are perfect, unwrinkled, and I wonder if he ever sweats. How can any man look so incredible all the time?

He moves around the room, affixing cufflinks to his remaining sleeve, then gives the sign he's ready.

"Let's go, shall we?" he says to me. His entourage knows their places and step effortlessly into their roles.

I walk dutifully to the door and notice with a pleased thrill that Dante and I walk ahead of the guards as if we're a couple.

Once downstairs, Flavio leaves only to reappear minutes later driving a black Escalade. I'm confused to see a car when the restaurant is so close, and I turn to Dante questioningly.

"I can't have you walking that far in those heels. That would be cruel and unusual punishment," he says, and the way he speaks with genuine concern, so different from his normal cold tone, makes my heart swell. Dante opens the door so I can slide over and let him in beside me.

"As if there is anything worse." I attempt the snappy retort as a joke, but it falls flat, and his piercing blue eyes darken.

"You have no idea the things I could do to torture you without ever touching you."

Fuck me.

My knees quiver and my core tightens. I'm wet just from his deep tone and what he implies, even though I have no clue what he's really talking about. I think he just threatened me... so why do I want him to tear my clothes off and ravage me right here, right now?

To avoid thinking about sex, I force myself to think of the beach, the clear Mediterranean water, and running along the shoreline chasing birds when I was a kid on family vacations.

A whiff of his tantalizing cologne brings me back to reality. This man drips sex with every word, with every look, and I recall that his body is sculpted like the David and is something to behold. From the intensity in his eyes and the way he has his hand on my knee, I'm sure if we were alone, we'd be fucking again, and I'd have his magnificent cock inside me.

I imagine his hands between my thighs and know I could have an orgasm if he so much as touched me there right now. When his thumb brushes the back of my knee, I take a deep breath, a dead giveaway that he's having an effect on me. He has to know that I won't be able to resist him were he to move his fingers higher.

No sooner do we pull away from the hotel than I find we are parked in front of what appears to be a fancy eating establishment. Two valets rush over to open our doors, and the maître d' rushes out to greet Dante by name. As I'm helped out of the car, I wonder if he owns this place too. I wouldn't be surprised. Any business establishment that handles a lot of cash is a good place to launder dirty money. I'm new to this world, but everyone knows that.

The evening is amazing as the air cools the warm streets, and light from the moon guides our walk to what is no doubt the most expensive place in the piazza. I stop dwelling on the darker side of his life as I'm introduced to the maître d' as Juliet, no last name. I take it as he doesn't want it known.

Who could my father be and what could be so seriously bad that even Dante doesn't want to mention his name? When this mystery man finds out I'm alive after twenty-one years, will my life be able to return to normal?

The maître d' ushers us to a table for six so we have room to spread out, and as I slide into the soft chair, I notice that the thick tablecloth covers my lap. For a brief moment, I think that maybe I could steal a steak knife as it looks pretty sharp, but to what end? I'm outnumbered.

I'm also in no immediate danger that I'm aware of. But the question I'm dying to ask, the one he keeps putting off answering, is who the hell is my dad and why is it such a secret?

I make a resolution to go along with the situation as long as I don't feel like I'm going to be shot. When I look up after smoothing my pretty dress down around my legs, I catch Dante's ocean-blue eyes and give him a small smile as a reward for letting me out of the hotel. Or is it just because he's looking happier than normal? No matter. It feels like a temporary truce.

He relaxes after a few glasses of rich Italian Syrah, and I have to admit more than I would like that the robust red wines he likes are agreeing with me. I can't fault him for loving his lifestyle of luxury.

He orders everything after asking me a few questions about what I like to eat and what's my favorite seafood. When the calamari arrives at the table, it's the freshest I've ever had.

Flavio and Riccardo converse in low tones while I sit at Dante's left.

"So, are you ever going to tell me who my dad is?" I blurt out abruptly.

He leans his sculpted torso toward me as his jacket strains against it and whispers, "We'll talk on the plane tomorrow."

I'm not happy with the answer, but instead of sulking, I rely on the wine to even out my emotions. I decide not to piss him off by pressing the issue. It would only ruin the evening for both of us.

Italian wines are notorious for sneaking up on a person, and this one is no different. I go over a silent Hail Mary in my head, hoping that the food arrives before I get too tipsy.

I don't know why I care what Dante thinks of me, but I'm smart enough to know that I don't want to throw up or fall asleep and look like a juvenile who can't hold her alcohol. Also, I need to be able to walk out of here on these stilts.

I lean forward, pluck another roll off the round plates, then rip it apart between my fingertips before dipping it in the olive oil. I nibble on the wet bread, and after it passes my lips, I gently suck the oil out of it, savoring the flavor in my mouth and letting it coat my tongue.

It's divine, and when I cast a look in Dante's direction as he talks in a low voice to Riccardo, I remember what his lips taste like.

The vision of his perfectly sculpted, kissable lips reminds me of how I sketched his face subconsciously a few days ago.

How many days has it been now? I'm losing track, but as long as I'm a hostage, it's important to remember. I return to looking at the ornate walls and the rounded arches leading from one room to another when I suddenly get the feeling I'm being watched.

I look up to discover warmth, not coldness, in Dante's eyes as he observes me like a sleek cat ready to pounce on its prey. He makes me feel like I'm the only person in the room, and for one brief moment, I'm infatuated with him when our eyes lock . . . until it hits me that he's not the least bit remorseful for plucking me from my life.

Our food arrives, carried in by two handsome waiters dressed in black tuxes and starched white shirts, who swirl around the table like a pair of silk scarves, flawless with their delivery and effortless with their movement. They move around us like perfectly choreographed dancers doing a pas de deux as they hand us our plates.

Soft Italian music is playing in the background as I take in the sight of my seafood dinner in front of me. It looks picture-perfect on the white china plate. It's way too much for one person, especially after all the bread and wine I've consumed.

By now, I can read Dante's mood from the color of his eyes, and I can tell by how dark they have turned that he's sending me a silent challenge to finish my dinner. He twists his pasta on his fork using a spoon to complete the perfect action before placing the first bite in his mouth, and his eyes briefly close as he enjoys the chef's signature dish.

I'm getting used to it, but I still marvel at the way that everywhere we go, the red carpet is rolled out for him. I wonder again if he owns this restaurant like he does the hotel.

A heavy man in his thirties walks to our table, getting a few handshakes from customers sitting at tables as he makes his way across the room. He's eager to talk to guests, and he stops to chat with Dante. He calls him Signor Micheli, and he expresses his hope that he is pleased with the food.

Dante reassures him that the food is the most incredible seafood he's had in a long time and that he couldn't be happier.

The man seems pleased with this, and with a slight bow, he says, "Ciao," before departing back to the kitchen.

The remainder of dinner passes without incident, and then it's home to the penthouse where I'm called over by Flavio to make a return text to Ava, who apparently has been asking how my family is doing and when I'll be back.

I draft the reply and show it to Flavio for his approval, and when he nods, I send it before handing the phone back to him. I tell her that I'd say I missed my art supplies, but I've been so busy the entire time, I haven't had the time to sketch anyway. I hope that sounds authentic.

Dante's eyes are steely when I bid everyone a good night and excuse myself for bed. I peel off my fancy clothes and discover that I'm wet between my legs. The man out there is driving me crazy, but I can't be the one to make a move. My observations have taught me that their world operates like a wolf pack—they stick together, and everyone is an alpha until they are outranked by a superior in the group.

And Dante is the alpha of all alphas, the don, and the one who I'm thinking of as I slide my fingers between my lower lips and rub my clit, caressing my breasts as I build to a crescendo and muffle my orgasm as I silently scream his name.

\* \* \*

When I wake in the morning, I momentarily forget where I am. Then it comes back to me—I'm the princess locked away in the tower. I dress casually in a Milano silk blouse and designer jeans and those cute sneakers before making my way into the sitting room.

Everyone is quiet when I walk in. I look at my captors and I can't read anything on their stoic and impassive faces, but I get the sense that something is going on.

We eat with little conversation. I sip my espresso, and then Dante tells me to pack as Flavio brings a large designer suitcase into my room.

"Harrumph," escapes under my breath. This isn't the way I saw this going down, but I want to keep all the things he bought me, so I go along with it.

We have a second car follow us to the airport, black like ours, and we make our way back to the jet.

I purposely behave so Dante won't have an excuse to deny me the information about my father today. I'm excited to find out who my dad really is since it seems to be the best-kept secret, right up there with whatever happened to the missing city of Atlantis.

The entourage disappears as we take off, and I'm a little disappointed to see that the Dante of yesterday has disappeared and the stranger with his cold looks and stiff posture has returned.

"So, what about my father?"

"This again," he complains.

"Yes, this again. You promised." It's a test to see if he keeps his word.

He sighs heavily. "All right, but you can't tell anyone. Telling your parents will put them in grave danger, capisci?"

"Sì." I shrug, but I'm reserving my real response based on what he tells me.

"Only Riccardo and I know, along with your father. It's to keep you safe, babe." His voice softens, and I begin to fall under the spell of his deep, hypnotic voice again.

"Go on."

"Your father is a rival don and my family's nemesis. We are enemies. His name is Gio Conti and he's not to be taken lightly. He's very dangerous and I'm negotiating your safety in exchange for him to uphold an agreement we made years ago about a business deal."

"Will I see him?"

"Probably. He wants to meet you. But he's not trustworthy, so we need to be careful." He brushes my arm with his slender, tanned fingers, as if lost in thought.

"You will keep the promise of silence, Juliet?"

"Yes," I reply briefly, and right now, I will because it's in my best interests for the time being. In the long run, well, I'll have to cross that bridge when I get to it.

I ask the question that has been bothering me as much as the one about my father's identity. "Why did he give me up?"

"I don't know, but your mother was one of his mistresses. He probably couldn't afford to divorce his wife as it was an arranged marriage. Plus, in my world, women and children are liabilities."

"I get that," I agree, and it crosses my mind I'm a liability to both Conti and Dante. It explains the somber faces and quiet voices on the plane.

"What happens next? I need to get back to school."

"I know. We're going to meet Conti, but I warn you, he's not a nice man. You may be too young to understand fully what he is, but I will keep you safe. This I promise you."

A chill runs up my spine. He's speaking so cryptically. I'm swimming around in his words and vocal cues, trying to decipher if he thinks the meet will go well or badly for us.

"I see why you're stressed. Meanwhile, I'm your leverage over him, to line your pockets with more profits. But what will become of me?"

"I don't know," he says simply, and when he looks at me, his eyes are soft and sincere. I could almost believe he cares, but I'm not sure he's capable of that emotion. He's walled off to everything and everyone from what I can see, and aside from our tryst yesterday, he doesn't seem interested.

I can't breathe. The mingling of his citrusy cologne mixed with an ocean breeze surrounds me. Combine that with this black suit and his slicked-back hair—and it's enough to make any woman cream in her pants, and I'm not far from it. God, if he keeps this up, I'm going to need a new vibrator.

# CHAPTER 17

## DANTE

*I* can't take my eyes off Juliet when I find her ready to go to dinner, nor can I do so when we arrive at the restaurant. But I can't make another move on her as doing so might mean death to her or to me. I'm more worried for her. I don't know which emotion runs stronger in Conti—the desire to protect her, like when he gave her up to be raised in anonymity, which took considerable fortitude and money, or his evil side, where he'd just as soon kill her as look at her, a sobering reminder of his infidelity that he would probably rather forget.

We had two more famiglia deaths just north of Rome, and I'm waiting for the local police to give me more details. I can't tell if they are another message sent by Conti or just a coincidence. Either way, it's better that I tighten my security now, so I have Riccardo take care of that before dinner.

The way Juliet makes eating her bread look like foreplay is driving me crazy, and I stir in my soft chair. I notice the wine is hitting her pretty hard. She must not drink much. She's so young, mamma mia, I remember that age. College was my time to have fun and play harder than I studied.

Conti not calling isn't good, so I send word to all the capos that

I want boots on the ground for intel on any unusual movements from Conti. He's like me; we're both skilled at moving in the shadows, but he's been doing it longer.

The plane ride is easy, and the private jet is made for quick travels with none of the fuss. I've played for a day and now it's time to get back to work in my office. I have meetings about condos that need permits, and I'm sure tons of calls to return as I check messages on my phone and send some texts.

Juliet is rather quiet during the flight after I tell her about her father. She looks surprised when I have her sit in the back seat while I sit in the front for the ride from the airport to my home. It's a little late to think of that now, but it's better if I don't mix business with pleasure again.

We enter the house, and I head to my room to change into a fresh shirt, pants, and a different pair of leather shoes without a word to Juliet. I call my secretary and have her line up meetings for the rest of the week.

No sooner am I off the call than my phone dings and it's Conti. He wants to meet his daughter, and I tell him tomorrow is good as I don't want to give him too much time to prepare. Now, I have to get Juliet ready for the meet. It's not the typical father-daughter reunion that most kids dream of, just the opposite. She's letting someone worse than the devil in and I'm the one who set up the reunion—a reunion that I'm now regretting.

I knock on her door, and as it's already open a crack, I push it the rest of the way open. She's standing in a cute swimsuit that shows off her body and I can't decide if I want to run to her or far, far away.

"We're meeting Conti tomorrow," I inform her.

She bends over to slip on her sandals. "What are they going to do to me?"

"Hopefully nothing. Maybe he simply wants to meet you after all these years. But, trust me, he's not the Micheli family."

How can I warn her about the worm of a man she's going to meet?

"I don't understand," she meekly replies.

I get it, this has all been thrust upon her very quickly. She barely knows anything about my world, her father's world, and suddenly, she's been dropped right into the middle of it.

"I'll catch up with you later," I say. As I turn to go, she asks me to wait and for some reason, I stop in my tracks.

Fuck. Why did I do that?

"You're sure you'll be able to keep me safe?"

"Yes." I lie. There is always a first for something, but I want tomorrow to go as planned.

She nods. "Umm... thank you for the sketchbooks and stuff." She shrugs her shoulders matter-of-factly like her life is normal.

But we both know we're kidding ourselves. This relationship is nowhere near normal, and neither is the magnetic energy between us. I need to abort.

"Hmm." And I really leave this time, as Riccardo is waiting at the door.

\*\*\*

I walk into an old building on the corner of a street that's around the corner from a secret condo I have in Florence. It's registered under my grandmother's maiden name, and no one will ever guess that I'm hiding certain assets under her name as in Italy, it's not normal for women to own such expensive pieces of real estate, especially if they are married.

Riccardo opens the door for me, and I walk into our office. It just has the bare necessities. I'm not here enough to justify extravagance, and anyone visiting me here knows what I have, so there's no need to impress.

It's easier to hide my wealth in plain sight, in assets, mergers, and land, rather than rubbing the elite's noses in it and showing off. Being low key and flying under the radar is the best way to hide from prying eyes.

"Ciao," I greet Maria, a woman in her forties who has been my secretary since the day I took over. She's quiet and loyal and does a good job. She's married, not that that keeps men from hitting on her daily. It's Italy—it's what we do.

"Ciao," she responds with a smile. "I sent your messages to your email. I'm trying to find out when the next city meeting is for zoning."

"Great," I respond, wondering who's looking for a payday this time.

"Ciao, come sta?" Looking up from his laptop, my brother, Sal, greets me. He'd better not be surfing porn sites like he normally does when he's supposed to be working.

"Va bene," I reply mechanically, but he's observant and notices something is off and follows me to my office at the end of a long hallway. I like being where I am because I can keep my back to the wall and see trouble coming. Take a corner office, and you'll never be cornered.

We're not as hands-on as we used to be, and it's easier to make legitimate money when we've been bankrolled by illegal gains. Like the hotel in Milan—it used to be run down, but the location was perfect, so I had it redone by our guys' construction companies as well as handing out a few contracts to non-connected companies as well.

I laundered the street money through the bar downtown by reporting the money as sales and then paying the taxes on it. I have more than one bar, so it adds up quickly.

I sit in my leather swivel chair and idly wonder what Juliet is doing right now, but I'd be a pussy to check on her.

Sal gets right to the point. "What's up, Dante?"

"I was out of town to visit Milan." I smile. "I can't have enough new suits."

"I know, only the best for you, and you have to be prepared to do business all the time," he chides me, but it's normal as we're very close.

I pause, then fix him with a curious look, trying to sound casual. "Are you seeing anyone?"

"Why do you ask? What's up?"

"Do I need a reason to care if my brother is seeing someone?"

He sits on the corner of my desk with one foot on the ground. "Yes, you do. It's odd. You never care about who we bring around, as long as it's not an informant," he whispers.

"Normally, that's true. I'm just taking an interest in you, brother, that's all." I flash him a quick smile to put him at ease.

"I'm not seeing anyone in particular right now, but I always have a few lined up, y'know?"

Boy, do I ever. My entire life, Sal has been the most sociable of all of us.

He's still friends with some of the guys we attended private school with here in Florence and he always knows where to go to be a part of the 'in' crowd. He's the one I use if I need to smooth over a work situation that I'm too frustrated to deal with calmly.

Funny how we work so well together, Babbo would be proud.

"What about you, Dante? No one special in your life yet?" It's an odd question. He knows I only do hookups, some just more extended than others.

"Same."

He takes the hint to change the subject and asks, "How was Milan?"

"Fantastic," I reply, "and our business arrangement with our friend in the south is progressing. I'll be meeting him to negotiate, and I hope he will see it our way."

"Hmm, good luck with that, brother. I don't envy you the big decisions." He gets up from my desk, stretches his arms, and wanders out of my office.

My brothers know of the plan to gain use of the port; they just aren't aware of the details of how I plan to accomplish it. Meeting Conte on Saturday is perfect, so I can be at Mama's for Sunday dinner and not raise suspicion. I can miss a Sunday dinner if I have to, but I'd rather not. It's the only interaction I have with my family outside of work.

I start to work on my computer as Riccardo hangs out in the break room and talks business with the associates. He will fill me in on all the chatter when he drives me home.

# CHAPTER 18

## JULIET

*I* wasn't expecting Dante to visit my room while I was putting on my new bikini. He looked great standing there in his fresh shirt, but he seemed a bit rattled to find me undressed. I made sure to bend over and put my sandals on, teasing him with a view of my ass. Call it payback for ignoring me since we got off the plane. The man is all about mixed signals, blowing hot one minute and cold the next, like an old boiler heater.

He disappeared before I could even finish putting on my shoes.

I want to cool off, so I grab a pool towel and head to the back-yard where I find a chaise lounge and lie down to absorb a few rays. When the sun gets to be too much, I take a dip in the warm water and do laps for some exercise. It seems each year the summers get hotter and last longer, but today, the temperature is perfect. I just wish Dante was here to enjoy the day with me.

I'll admit it—I miss him. We had such a great day yesterday. I miss his cologne, his presence in a room, and the tiny smile he rarely shows anyone. And when I manage to coax one out of him, I feel like the luckiest girl in the world. I don't know why I want to make him happy, but I do.

Done with the sun, I shower and change into linen Capri pants and a matching pink top. I love the way the pants flatter my curves, and the color looks good with my tan.

Noticing my hair is still damp from the shower, Enzo asks the woman mopping the floors to bring me a hairdryer. Minutes later, she drops it off, only to disappear again before I can thank her. I chuckle to myself, convinced this place has trapdoors by the way people appear and disappear.

After I finish drying my hair, I look for a TV and find one in a room away from the main area of the house. It's a less formal room with a dark tan leather sofa and has an old-school masculine vibe that makes me wonder if some of the furnishings belonged to Dante's dad. The entire length of one wall is a built-in bookcase filled with books as well as family photos, and I decide to be nosy and try to learn more about Dante—if that's even possible.

I pick up one framed black and white photo that looks to be of him with some other boys on a soccer field. He was a cute kid, but that doesn't surprise me. The people in the vintage wedding photos, I assume, are his parents or grandparents. There are enough books to fill a library, and most are old and dusty, almost as if the maid doesn't clean in here nearly as often.

I put the picture of him back on the shelf and I realize that a casual observer would not see these pictures from the doorway. They are practically hidden on these bookshelves, tucked away from the rest of the house. What else is he hiding in this mansion? I wonder if there's a safe room, and if so, if it's built for one or two.

Finished with my snooping, I settle on the couch to watch TV on a screen so large it fills the entire wall that opposes the book-cases, leaving no room to spare.

Come to think of it, I haven't seen any personal pictures of him anywhere else around the house. Or, for that matter, pictures of family celebrations or summer vacations. Until I came into this room, there was no evidence that he lived here.

I appreciate that I'm allowed to wander around the house. With so many guards outside, it would be pointless to try to get away anyhow. In these hills, it would be ridiculous and only hurt me in the long run because then he wouldn't trust me. The last thing I want is to be tied to a chair with zip ties again.

Dante has told me so many horrible things about my dad, but I'll keep an open mind and decide for myself. I may be naïve and inexperienced, but I'm a good judge of character.

I settle into the sofa, its softness so inviting I fall asleep.

"What are you doing in here?"

Startled, I wake up and see Dante looming over me with Enzo behind him in the doorway.

"What?" I'm still foggy from my nap and need a minute to think.

"Who gave you permission to be in my study?"

"I didn't know I couldn't be in here. I'm sorry." It doesn't seem a big deal to me.

"Well?" He waits for me to move and gestures to the door.

"You don't have to be such an ass about it," I snap. Crap, I can't believe I spoke to him that way. He demands respect, and I just totally crossed a line.

"What?"

"Nothing, I'm sorry." Sheepishly, I get up to go back to my room, but as I pass him, he grabs my arm.

"What are you up to?"

"Nothing." I flare as I yank my arm back. "What's wrong with you?"

He releases my arm and lets me pass. After I push past Enzo, I can hear Dante barking at him, and I feel bad. Enzo may be a foot soldier moving up the ranks but he has been the nicest to me out of the three guards.

Walking past the kitchen, I see the woman from this morning, the one who cleans. Apparently, she cooks too because she's in the kitchen stirring something on the stove that must be delicious. My stomach reminds me I skipped lunch, so I make a detour and introduce myself. She tells me her name is Rosario and hands me a cup of Italian wedding soup.

I'm hungry enough, so I finish all of it, and it's good, but honestly, my mother's is better. Now, I want something sweet to eat and open the freezer, looking for gelato. I find one in the back and pull it out.

I'm opening the container when Dante walks into the kitchen. "I was going to eat that," he grunts, peeved.

"Hmm, well, I was going to share it with you, but now, I think not," I saucily reply, tempting fate. That will teach him to ignore me all day.

"This might call for a spanking if you don't want to obey," he threatens.

That wouldn't be so terrible.

I pick up a spoon and dig in, taking a scoop and putting it in my mouth, licking it like it's his hard cock and moaning ever so slightly. Rosario continues to stir her soup and keeps her head down.

"You'll regret that," he warns, but his eyes no longer frighten me. If anything, instead of anger, I see passion.

I step closer to him, teasing him, "I thought you said you don't like lemon flavor, so why do you have it?"

"I love lemon! I just don't like mixing flavors," he protests.

"Well?" I purse my lips around the curve of the spoon and swallow.

"You're being a brat," he says, standing with his legs apart and arms folded across his chest.

I walk closer, taunting him with another scoop of gelato. "I guess I am."

He grabs my hand holding the spoonful of gelato and brings it to his mouth. We're so close, I feel the heat from his body and his breath on my face.

He barks at Rosario and Enzo to leave, and they scurry.

I don't flinch as his hand tightens around my wrist. "You're hurting me."

"I thought you enjoyed it," he growls, and he bends me over the kitchen table and pulls down my pants and my lacy panties, leaving me completely exposed. Then I feel a resounding smack on my ass and feel a sting that hurts and excites me at the same time. The sting gives way to a slow-burning sensation that I think I could learn to enjoy.

He pulls me up roughly and spins me around, pinning me up against the wall with his body and holding my wrists over my head with one hand while his other slides down my abdomen until it reaches the opening of my wet pussy. He roughly shoves his fingers into me at the same time as his mouth finds mine, crushing my lips with urgency. I almost come right there.

A soft moan escapes his throat as his fingers go deeper, moving fast and ruthlessly inside me, causing me both pain and pleasure, so much so that I stiffen and stand on my toes. I'm sure he could pick me up like this if he wanted.

His pressure doesn't let up and I'm gasping for air under his deep kisses as I feverishly kiss him back. We're like two lovers separated by war, who haven't seen each other for years and have finally been reunited.

He lets go of my wrists and my hands grab the back of his neck, my nails digging into his flesh in response to being lifted off the floor an inch or two as his fingers work their magic deep inside of me.

His hard cock is pressed against my thigh, eager to fill my pussy. Dante rubs my clit just enough to make me moan from the friction and the anticipation. I'm surfing on a wave of pleasure brought on by his skilled fingers and tongue.

Keeping his knee between my thighs, he unzips his trousers, releasing his cock that is the size of a zucchini, he's so hot for me. He doesn't give me long to admire it. Grabbing my hips, he thrusts into me. I do not protest or fight him off. I want this as much as he does.

I love how strong and powerful he is, breaking the rules, and oh my sweet baby Jesus, he has both hands under my butt cheeks and knows exactly how to move me, finding my G-spot and whatever other buried treasure is in there that no other man has found.

As my orgasm builds, I clench onto his shoulders and his mouth wraps around one breast, teasing the nipple. Right when I'm ready to explode, he gives it a nip that sends me over the edge and I scream out, releasing my sleeping dragon as I climax loud enough for anyone on the grounds to hear me.

Dante pumps faster and faster, holding my butt cheeks in his strong hands as he comes inside me with a loud groan. His head slumps on my shoulder, and I rest my head against him as he lets my feet touch the floor, but he continues to hold me as I'm too weak to stand on my own.

We stand entwined until my legs feel steady enough to support me, and he lets go so I can pull up my panties and find my pants.

He leaves without a word.

# CHAPTER 19

## DANTE

*R*osario serves the four of us dinner, and Juliet is too quiet. I pour her wine and she takes only small bites of her food. I wonder if I fucked her too hard an hour ago in this very room.

Riccardo and Flavio joke about a girl they saw in Milan, and instead of adding to the comments about how big her breasts were and how Flavio would have fucked her in an alley given half a chance, I clear my throat and they stop.

The guys sense my foul mood. Riccardo leaves immediately after dinner while Flavio waits for Juliet, who decides to follow me into my den.

"What?" I'm not in the mood for small talk.

"What's the deal with my dad, my biological one?" She sits on the corner of the table, letting her leg tease me by its sheer presence, dangling within my reach.

A couple of good fucks and she's learned how to manipulate my baser needs into something she wants. So typical of a woman.

"What do you mean?" I flip off the TV on the wall and give her my full attention. "We're meeting him tomorrow, his side won't have any weapons, just don't get too close. Simple."

"Why don't you like him?" she asks.

"Long family history."

"Dante," she protests.

"I can't tell you." I try again to brush her off, but I know it's useless.

She gives me a look I can't deny; that tiny smile of hers with perfect teeth and perfect lips, lips I kissed so passionately just over two hours ago.

I pull a file out of my desk and hand it to her. "Here."

She opens it and her eyes grow wide as she looks through it. I'm worried she's going to throw up her dinner.

"He does... this?"

"That, and more. I refuse to take part in human trafficking. He started that years ago, but we didn't want the heat. We were sharing the docks at the time. It ended up nasty, with each side killing a son of the don at the time."

"Your dad?"

"His brother, my uncle."

"And one of my dad's brothers?"

"Yes."

She sets the file aside.

"So, this thing with me is to even the score?"

"Somewhat, but more importantly, I'm trying to get use of the docks. I need them as our most productive port was taken out by last year's earthquake. So, we went over your family history, looking for a weakness to exploit. Your dad has a thing for young women and a history of being unfaithful. I knew there had to be illegitimate kids somewhere."

"Me."

"Yes, maybe others, I don't know, but you have to understand he is a real psycho and he's not above killing his own kids if he needs to. In our world, family makes one weak, which is why I'll never marry, never have a girlfriend."

"Weak?" she sounds confused.

"Yes. It's not like the old days when family members were off-limits. This world is rough. You'd never fit in."

"My mother? Where is she?"

"She disappeared. Her name was Isabella Gambini, and she was a member of a rival mafia family back then that has all but disappeared these days. There's no trace of her. But that's the name we were given that led us to you."

"Then, why didn't my dad look for me?"

"Maybe he tried. He's been married for over thirty years but has a new mistress every week. Please promise me you'll never trust anything that comes out of his mouth."

"Okay," she says.

I can tell they're just words. A young woman like her, with so little real-world experience, can't possibly know what it's like to deal with men like him.

"You say that, but have continually tell yourself that you can't trust him. Everything out of his mouth is a lie, all of his business partners end up either dead, or in prison, or broke."

"Then why do you want to do business with him?"

"It's not the same thing. We run our stuff through the same port, so we're like two ships passing in the night. That's how it used to be, and these days, we Italians have to stick together as there are so many new factions and upstart gangs out there. It's in our best interests that we not go after each other."

"Hmm." Her demure face is sullen. Suddenly, she looks up.

"Do you think he'd hurt me?"

"Yes," I reply promptly, and the answer makes her jump off the desk.

"He would?"

"Oh, of course, that's what I'm saying, he's not to be trusted. Look out."

"What about you? What if he knew about us?"

"Let's just say it wouldn't be good. So, behave, Juliet." His deep voice serves as a warning.

"You screwed me over for your own gains," she accuses me flatly.

"I can't help it. Any man in my place would make the same move."

"Enough, I don't want to hear any more." Her nostrils flare as she stands, staring me down. "I want my life back." And as if a switch has flipped, she declares, "I don't want to meet him. If I don't meet him, I can go back to life the way it was before you kidnapped me."

She smiles triumphantly, like she's found her solution and feels she's in control of her own life for a full minute before she reads my face.

"You promised him something." Her voice falters.

"A meet, with you, to seal the deal."

"So, I'm paying the price for your lavish penthouse and cars and —" She runs out of material objects too soon.

"Look, it's a lot to take in, and I'm sorry, truly, but it needs to be done." I take the folder from her, put it in my desk, lock it with a push of a button, and get up.

My wall of indifference is up. I can't let emotions and consequences of what this will do to her life interfere with my family's objective. The port is worth billions in new revenue for us as they run it like a military operation, right under the noses of authorities who are either bought or threatened.

"I thought you were better than this, Dante," she whispers before she turns to go, but she stops at the door. "You'll not have me again. I deserve more . . . so much more."

I can hear her voice waver and I can tell she's close to tears, but she refuses to let me see them. With that, she squares her shoulders and walks from the room with her head held high to turn in for the night.

In my heart, I have a bad feeling, but a deal with the worst devil in the world is still a deal. The meet has to happen or war is certain.

I poked the bear, now the bear wants more than the bear can have, and he might have to be put down.

How did I get into this mess? Women and children were never on my list of targets until I discovered Conti's secret. I run my hand over my stubbled chin. My phone vibrates and it's Alessia. I look at the name for a couple of rings, then answer.

"Sure, I'll be on the road in a few and let you know where to find me."

She's lonely and I let her down hard the last time we spoke. I think if I see her and tell her I've found someone else, even if that's a lie, she'll move on. Sometimes people just need a push in the right direction.

I call out to Flavio, to let him know I'll be back in a few hours, and he acknowledges.

I go to the old garage beside the house, open the door, and I smile. Time for my yellow Lamborghini Aventador.

I slide into it and listen to the engine purr as I throw it in gear. This will be a good way to take my mind off the only woman I can't have, the woman who could bring down my empire, the woman who makes my cock jump while I'm just watching her shopping for Christ's sake. The woman who dares to challenge me. The woman who secretly makes me smile, but I have to hide it to keep her safe, to keep us both safe.

My headlights swivel around the narrow turns as I make my way down the mountainside. Oncoming traffic is honking at me for drifting over the median, and I cross back into my lane. One would think I had a death wish, but it's just what I do to feel a thrill that's not related to work.

Now, as I take each dangerous bend, I'm kicking myself for ruining Juliet's life. No matter what the outcome is, she will never have a normal existence and will be forever looking over her shoulder as long as Conti is alive. And it's all my fault for setting this in motion.

I pull into a pub that I like in downtown Florence. The locals frequent it, and there aren't many tourists. It's a casual pizza, beer, and wine joint, and I know Alessia would rather go to a fancier place where we can be seen, but I'm just not in the mood.

We greet each other with a kiss on the cheek and take a seat.

"Dante," she puts her hand on mine, "I've missed you. What have you been up to?"

I spread my hands in appeal. "Work. It's been very busy. I got some new contracts for renovating an apartment building, and my brother got a few new clients redoing multimillion condos along the river."

"That's great, but you need a vacation." She lets her shoulders slump forward as she gives a tiny laugh, a subtle suggestion that she wants to have a weekend shopping getaway with me.

It's fine, we've known each other a few years, so she needs to get something out of our arrangement before I cut her loose. I'm just not that into her anymore.

It's hard to focus on the conversation with Alessia. The afternoon with Juliet keeps replaying in my head like a slow-motion movie, with me grabbing her thighs, lifting her, and holding her against the wall. I'm quite impressed with my muscles to hold her up that long and I'm amazed that I didn't break my cock because we were going at it so hard. Truth be told, I found it exciting to dominate her so much. Maybe I'm more of a control freak than I imagined.

"Let's go out, the night's young." Alessia nudges me.

"You want a beer?" She knows me, so this will tell her I've made up my mind that I want to hang here for now.

I'm not sure why I even agreed to see her this evening. Maybe it's because I need to distance myself from Juliet, and I talked myself into the belief that if I dipped my *[dip]* in someone else, I'd forget her. Not a chance. As I slide back into my chair, I rest my index finger on my chin and take in the woman sitting across from me. She's perfect, model quality, and I should be putting a ring on her finger, but I can't.

I want someone real, someone with goals, that special someone currently sleeping under my roof. And now, I have to figure out how to not only keep her for myself but also keep her safe.

Tonight, I have to end things with Alessia. She knows it's coming; she'd be crazy or deluded not to see the writing on the wall.

I think I'll stay at my condo here in Florence for the night. I'm craving solitude. I rarely stay here. Babbo put it in my name when I turned eighteen, but I went off to college shortly after that. He told Mom he just bought it, but I know he had it forever and he had more than a few mistresses over the years.

# CHAPTER 20

## JULIET

*I* watch TV with Enzo in the room. He alternates pacing back and forth with moving in and out of the room, checking in with others via the earpiece and the mic on his shirt. He means serious business, and I wonder if he's the head of the guards.

Once again, I'm struck by how elegant the men all look when they are assigned to be with me or Dante, even if they have guns strapped into holsters under their jackets.

Some women might be afraid of the guns, but not me. Dad used to take me hunting on Christmas Day in the country, and I'm a pretty good shot if I do say so myself.

I don't know where the man of the house is tonight. Odd, he's been here every night up till now. I ask Enzo if he's okay.

"He's fine," he assures me.

I resign myself to the fact that he must be out on business, and I return to my room to sketch a scene I begged the guys to let me take a picture of while in Milan. It's such a beautiful city, I just had to draw something to capture the moment in my sketchpad as well as in my mind.

I go to the dresser where I keep my art supplies, and when I get closer, I see a small box on top of it. The blue is unmistakable.

Curious, I pick up the rectangular iconic blue box with 'Tiffany' stamped on the top. I pry the box open carefully with all the anticipation of a child on Christmas morning and clap my hand over my mouth when I see the watch, with the classic blue face, silver hands, and black leather band.

How did he know I wanted to know the time? Without my phone on me, I'm at the mercy of using the sun and buildings as a makeshift sundial.

I eagerly fasten it around my slender wrist, and it crosses my mind that he might be trying to buy my submission. But if submission feels like it did when he slammed me up against the kitchen wall, I'd be absolutely okay with that.

***

Just as I'm descending the elegant steps in the morning light, the front door opens and Dante breezes in, oblivious to the fact that I've been worried sick that he's been out all night. I approach him, and as I do, I can't ignore the overpowering perfume on his suit jacket. It's so strong I'm about to choke on it. It's not just the odor; it's the fact that he was with someone else and that our trysts in the kitchen and in Milan obviously meant nothing to him when they meant something, no—everything, to me. Apparently, he's content to move from one conquest to another.

"Did you fall into a pool full of rose water?" I glare at him.

"Ciao," he greets me, impervious to my furrowed eyebrows and judging gaze, and brushes past me.

"Ciao," I fling at his back. I'm sure it falls on deaf ears. He's already on the second floor. I'm assuming he needs a shower to rinse off that stink.

I shrug my shoulders and head to the kitchen to see what

Rosario is up to. She's heating an espresso as I sail into the room and plop at the table.

"Long night?" she asks, perhaps noticing my sour look, so at odds with the cheery pink pantsuit I'm wearing.

"No longer than usual." We chat and I ask her how she's doing and if I can help her cook today, as I'm bored. This waiting around is growing old.

Today is the day we're to meet my biological father, and I have no details yet, nothing about the time, place, or how long we'll meet.

Flavio should be here any minute if the usual routine is being followed, so maybe I can ask him if he knows anything. I find that even though Flavio is very tall and intimidating, I feel like I can ask him for help, within reason. Enzo, on the other hand, reminds me of a Mexican cartel soldier. Too militant for my liking, but that's his job. You don't belong in a mafia family if you can't do the necessary jobs, and I'm sure he'll carry out orders.

"What's the matter?" Rosario asks as I sulk into my palm with my elbow on the table.

"Niente."

"Ah, boy problems." She gives me an all-knowing smile.

"No, not boy problems." I'm not lying.

"Boy problems, I can see it all over your face. My dear girl, Italian men are never faithful, you know that," she says, not unkindly.

"Sì," I agree tiredly. It's common for men to have mistresses, so why would Dante not have many? He's an eligible bachelor and he probably has women all over the world.

Today, I meet my dad, a man whom I know nothing about except, according to Dante, he's the worst kind of criminal there is. I should look him up on the internet. Why didn't I think of that before?

I go searching for Dante, but he's not down yet, and I'm not chasing after him. My legs are closed now that I know he's been with someone else. Italian men like to have someone on the side, I know that, but that's never going to fly with me.

I ask Riccardo, who just blew in, if he can look up my father online for me.

"What are you looking for, an arrest record?" he asks.

I shrug. "I just want to know what the world thinks of him."

"You might not like it. He's flashy and not like us when it comes to trying to stay undiscovered."

"I think I can handle it." I sit beside him on the couch in the formal living room that shows no wear on the cushions, and I wonder again if Dante has any friends.

I peer over his arm to see his phone screen when Dante bursts onto the scene.

"What are you doing? We're meeting Conti today, or did you forget?" he snaps at us. "Let's go, we have to leave. We have a long drive ahead of us."

I've never seen him so on edge. All his calm demeanor with underlying ruthlessness goes flying out the window as he barks at the guards next. Riccardo tries to direct him to the task at hand which is getting us into the Rover. Eventually, we get ourselves organized, and half the entourage is in front of the Rover while the other half is following behind.

I'm sure Dante is Conti's least favorite person in the world, and I feel like an Italian princess who has a bounty on her head, but our entourage shows strength, unity, and power. I just hope these windows are all bulletproof. The subdued mood in the vehicle isn't relaxing, to say the least, and I wish Dante would lighten up.

"I just wanted to look up my dad," I whisper. "Riccardo did nothing wrong."

"You don't have to explain his behavior, or yours, to me," he says curtly. "But you need to remember your place here. And don't ask too many favors. You flash those dark brown eyes of yours with a tiny smile pursed on your lips, and well, it's hard to refuse," he grumbles, and he turns his head away to look out the window.

We're moving at a good clip given the mountainous roads that are all curves and sharp turns. I can tell we are moving closer to Tuscany as I start to see vineyards, and soon, we are passing old trucks filled with grapes that have just been picked. We're near my hometown, in fact, we will pass it on our way to Siena.

"Do we have time to stop?" I ask my captor.

"Not a good idea with all the vehicles. I'm sure we've received too much attention as it is. Maybe on the way back, I can have them hang back and we can make a quick stop. But no promises."

"Okay. Thank you," I say meekly. I have to remember I'm only alive at his will.

I'm not even sure why I want to stop. Mama would never recognize me now in all my designer clothing and I will feel like I have betrayed my humble upbringing if I buy into his luxurious expensive lifestyle where he can purchase anything he wants, except me. I'm not for sale.

We roll through my town of Greve and pass old trucks with wagons that are filled to the brim with grapes for wine. Picking the grapes is a job most teenagers do in high school before they move on to other things.

"So, who is she?" I ask without preamble.

"Who?" He turns to face me with a piercing gaze, and now I regret asking him.

"Whoever bathed you in her perfume last night."

"Just an old friend, nothing for you to be concerned about."

"I will never willingly submit to being just another mistress for you," I snarl.

"I know."

"Then, why did you do it?"

I look out the window and try to act like everything is fine, but it's not. I'm deeply wounded by how casual and uncommitted he is to everything except this long-standing feud with my family. A feud that I never asked to be a part of, and one I never knew of, but now I'm living daily.

"You've got nothing to fear. She's a friend, that's all."

"Ha, friends with benefits." I shift away from him on the back seat.

"I don't answer to you, or anyone else," he counters. Then he falls silent.

I'm resolved not to speak first, and I know that probably makes him happy. He likes his solitary world, alone, with no complications, no drama. I'm sure his job has plenty of all that, and he shoulders it alone. He might consult with Riccardo, maybe others, but so far, with me, he's a sealed vault.

We enter Siena and the drivers start looking for parking as we bump over the cobbled streets and approach the piazza. When we get out, the guards are on high alert, and Dante holds my hand as we continue on foot to what I assume is the Duomo di Siena, judging from the architecture and the stunning mosaic floor. We are unarmed as we make our way through security.

My anxiety is through the roof. Standing in the church with Dante and his entourage is the least of it. It's not just the two of us or four of us anymore. Men are arriving in similar vehicles from all directions, and I don't know if they are on our side or our enemies. I suddenly feel cold despite the heat of the day and dread overwhelms me. How do I know I can trust Dante? Or Conti?

Dante takes my hand and begins to walk with me, but I find my feet glued to the ground.

He turns. "What's the matter? This is not a time to be obstinate."

"I...I can't move." The paralyzed look I give him makes his hard exterior crack.

"Oh, Juliet." He moves closer to me and wraps his arms around me. He feels me shudder against him and uses one hand to push my hair back as a father would if they were soothing a hurt child.

"I don't know if I can do this," I start, and he drops a small kiss on my lips.

"You're fine, baby. I promise you," he assures me, and with an arm around my shoulders, he walks again. This time, I find I am able to go with him.

"We won't have guns inside, but my men are everywhere."

"So are Conti's."

"True. It's something we have to do from time to time. I'm sorry, but it is necessary. Come, Princess, it will be fine."

We start walking. No doubt Conti's men are doing the same thing.

# CHAPTER 21

## DANTE

*I* go crazy when I stumble into the living room to find Riccardo and Juliet sitting so close. I trust Riccardo with my life, but nonetheless, I can't help but go berserk.

Riccardo is a father figure to me and surely more than old enough to be Juliet's. This jealousy is new and unfamiliar to me. I chalk it up to a stressful day that I can't wait to be over, even though it's barely started.

We have a long drive to the meet and I'm on edge all through it. There are many meetings like this in the history books where one or the other side gets shot. I promised Juliet I'd keep her safe and I will do everything I can to keep that promise.

When she asks me about my mistress, I can't tell her that I don't have any feelings for Alessia. Friends, sure, but I don't feel more for her. It's nothing like the hot attraction I'm trying to stifle with Juliet.

It's getting harder and harder to hide the attraction, and I'm sure Riccardo has picked up on it by now. It's normally not up to him to challenge me on what I do, but at this point, he should. It involves the mission we're on.

Juliet occupies my mind constantly, and it's not like me to let anyone get this close to me. The long ride sitting beside her is exhausting as I yearn to caress her tanned leg, and I can't.

She must have similar feelings if she's jealous of Alessia, but her dark eyes can hide so much. I can tell she's not used to trusting herself or men. Now that I know she was adopted, it might explain the issues she has connecting with people she hasn't known for very long. Friends, to go out, sure, but she's never had a long-term serious boyfriend. I have the file on her with details of her entire life. It's my job. I'm sure she'd view it as an invasion of privacy, and I smile to myself at that.

I say a silent prayer after I get Juliet to walk toward the Duomo. This is actually one of my favorite churches in all of Italy. At times, I feel regret that I'm not a practicing Catholic, but my work comes first, and I'm not going to add being a hypocrite to my considerable list of sins.

We make our way through security to a safe area in the back, where we can keep an eye on who is coming in, and we wait. Barely a few minutes pass before I locate Conti coming in with four men. His obnoxious, flashy suit makes him look more like a throwback to the seventies than the don of a powerful mafia family in southern Italy. I'm sure he's wearing a top designer, but there is nothing subtle about the man.

Juliet stiffens beside me, so I casually place my hand on the small of her back for support without broadcasting it to the other side. As Gio Conti approaches, we shake hands, though it's not the same dismissive shake he used before he knew I had Juliet. But I know better than to ever underestimate my enemy, and I will never let my guard down around him.

His eyes are flint.

"Hello, Dante."

"Gio." I take his hand and nod.

He looks at Juliet and extends his hand. She takes it, trying not to be tentative about it, but I can tell she's not getting good vibes.

"Hello," she says as neutrally as possible. He raises her hand to his lips and kisses it.

"I've longed to meet you for so many years but never could find you. I have to thank Dante for that." He turns to me and adds, "You never said how you found her."

"It doesn't matter, does it?" Not a chance I'm telling him that.

"No," he concedes as he returns his gaze to Juliet. "I guess it doesn't."

I'm not convinced he won't torture someone for the information, but I hope it won't be me.

"Let's sit," he suggests, and his arm sweeps to indicate a bench in a church pew.

We take up three rows, the three of us in one and our men both in front and behind us.

"Juliet, tell me, how was your life growing up?"

"Fine, good life, couldn't ask for better parents."

"Where do you live now?"

I decide to break this off. "Enough with the twenty-one questions, Gio. I followed up on our deal and now, I expect you to uphold your end."

"What's a few questions going to hurt, eh?" The way he's holding Juliet's hand in his is creeping me out. It's bordering on a sexual predator vibe, and I want this to be over quickly.

He catches my warning look and turns his attention from Juliet to one of his goons. "Raphael," he says, snapping his fingers, and a man behind him delivers an envelope.

"Here's my offer. I'm taking a little more of a cut, but you won't be disappointed. You'll have the use of our services getting out of the port as well as the personnel we've got on the payroll."

I take the envelope from him and look over the agreement. I can live with it. Now, I just want to get out of here before he tries to rope me or Juliet into something else.

"You must come visit me at my estate, dear." His oily voice is testing my limits.

My skin is crawling, and Juliet looks absolutely traumatized.

"I think we need to be going. Juliet has other plans today and we just wanted to make good on our promise to give you a chance to meet your daughter."

"So fast?" he complains, "I've only gotten a few minutes." But he knows in our world the meets are never long, especially in tense situations like ours. No need to fan the flames between old enemies.

Nevertheless, he tries one more time. "Juliet, come with me. I can take care of you, and you'll have a good life. I can give you everything you desire."

"I'm fine, really. It was so nice to meet you." Even I can tell she's lying.

"I don't think you understand, you're my daughter and I'm taking you home. There aren't many people I take 'no' from." He looks her in the eyes before glancing up at me.

"She's taken. We're engaged," I suddenly pipe up. It's the only thing I think he might accept in order to save face. He's older, so it might fly for the moment.

He sizes me up in a new light. "I thought I felt a vibe between you both, but . . . well, well . . . the Contis and the Michelis at long last."

I can't place his grin. Is it real? Or is it a ruse to buy himself time?

Conti stands and gives Juliet a hug that lasts way too long for my liking. It seems to take an eternity before he finally turns to go. We make our way out of the pew and head to a side entrance as planned. Our cars pull up immediately in response to Riccardo's text to our drivers.

"Go." I pull open the heavy door on the vehicle and hurry Juliet inside. I slide in after her as Riccardo gets in the front even as the others are returning to their SUVs. Once we are all safely locked inside, I allow myself a sigh of relief.

"Are you okay?" I ask Juliet, who's clipping her seatbelt.

"Yes," she says, trying to shake it off, but I know her better and can tell she's still rattled.

"Well, that's over." I sit back and straighten my jacket as the air conditioning kicks up to cool me.

"But is it?" Juliet whispers. "Will we have to see him again?"

"Probably not. He liked what he saw, but time will tell." Then I turn my attention to Riccardo. "We need to be careful when we start up at the port. All eyes and ears open extra wide. Any sign of trouble, we get out of there."

"Understood," Riccardo agrees from the front seat.

I slide my hand closer to Juliet and she takes it. Her hand is cold and might even still be trembling a little.

"You were right, he's creepy. Gave me chills."

"Yeah."

I squeeze her hand, and she squeezes back. We both realize we're in this together for survival now.

More importantly, I take it to mean that we're fine and she knows I didn't cheat on her last night. Sometimes a man just needs some space to clear his head. I'll have to show her my place downtown one day. It could be nice to stay there together.

"What's next?" she asks, and I can tell she's overwhelmed.

"We'll take it one day at a time, but tomorrow is Sunday, and my mother always hosts family dinner on Sunday. She's always on me to get a wife. I guess it's time to make her happy."

"Are we doing that?"

"I think we should. I'm your protection against your dad. After we're engaged, you can have your phone back. I'm sorry it's taken so long, but I couldn't risk anything going wrong."

"I understand. By the way, I never thanked you for the gorgeous watch. It helped a lot."

I rub my thumb back and forth across the back of her hand while the guys continue to communicate over their headsets to make sure we're not being followed.

I'll be relieved when this day is over. And for once, seeing my family tomorrow is actually something I'm looking forward to.

But we have to stop downtown first. If we're going to sell this, Juliet is going to need a huge fucking ring.

# CHAPTER 22

## JULIET

*S*unday morning. It's odd to go from being the girl no one knew existed to dating the most handsome and richest man in Florence. It's a lot to take in. My head is spinning, but I know I'm safer here with Dante than with anyone else—so much for having a boring life.

"I want you to move into my room," Dante mentions casually. He's standing in the hallway upstairs wearing a pair of Lucky jeans that hit him in all the right places. I never knew what lusting over someone felt like before, but I do now. I would love him to throw me up against the wall again, but we have to get ready to meet his family this afternoon.

I'd protest moving into his room, but when I look at the mammoth of a rock on my finger to sell the engagement, I can't exactly deny him. Even though the ring came without an official proposal, I'm not at all upset as we don't love each other. Lust after each other, yes, but I can't comprehend how I'm going to fit in his world. I also don't want to know all the things he does and considers to be all in a day's work.

"Okay."

"Get Rosario to help you," he suggests.

I don't mind Rosario helping me, I like her.

But as far as Dante goes, I still have so many questions. Can I trust him to be faithful to me? Can I live with the fact that the business will always come first? Will he ever share all his secrets with me?

With the craziness of the past week behind us, I can finally reach out to my adoptive family and Ava, which is amazing. But part of my new reality is if I go somewhere, anywhere, I need protection to accompany me. I don't trust Gio Conti. Putting all their family differences aside, I can understand why Dante doesn't like the man and would do anything to keep me safe from him. However, what kind of a life am I going to have?

Riccardo is putting the business plans into effect for the port. I know Dante will always be on edge with that arrangement. Other than that, I would be happy not to get involved in the business and only have him share details on a need-to-know basis. But he seems to want to get me involved in some capacity.

"I know you like art, so would you be interested in working for the company? You mentioned that you applied for waitressing jobs, but I can't have you doing that. What about studying graphic design or interior design? I think you would be a real asset and, of course, I know I can trust you completely."

I never dreamed I'd be able to use my creativity like that. Who wouldn't want such an opportunity? I'd love the chance to have a real job that pays me decent money. As well, I could be financially independent instead of feeling like a kept woman.

But I have doubts. "I don't know if I'm good enough."

How can I compare to the team he must already have in place? I don't want to be given a job just because I'm Dante's wife. I know Dante likes to have the best of everything, and that includes his employees.

"You'll be fine," he reassures me as he ducks back into his room, and I follow. He pulls on a casual tee in a bright blue that brings out the color of his eyes. They are such an unusual color that anyone would instantly focus on his eyes, but I like to take in the entire package. I can tell he works out as his torso is toned, and he must use the pool as he has a tan, and that small waistline is just ridiculous.

"Thanks for the new phone to go with my phone privileges," I venture as he buzzes around his room. Our room.

"Don't mention it. I'm glad you like it, and it's the least I could do."

"It means a lot that I can call my parents and Ava."

"Good. We'll have to sort out your schooling. Think about it, decide if you want to get your degree or work for the company full-time. I'm happy to pay all your expenses if you want to finish school. Either way, I'm here to help." He slides on his Italian loafers.

God, even his feet are perfect.

"I'll think about it, thanks."

"We also have to start making appearances at events. I'm donating money to your university, so there will be a photo and press conference later this week. That will probably be the first one."

"Money? Really?" And then I realize our picture will be splashed everywhere and my parents still don't know.

"Oh, yeah, I had planned on it since before I knew you went there. Meeting you that day was just coincidental," he continues, putting a small wallet in his pocket and grabbing his cell phone. "Oh, and you need more clothes."

"What? I have tons."

"Not suitable for the events we'll be going to. And you'll have a personal driver, but if you want your own car, I can arrange that too."

"Dante, I appreciate all this, but are you going to micromanage my entire life?"

He comes toward me as his eyes darken. "You are my fiancée and I promised to keep you safe. You will never go anywhere without an escort, is that understood?"

I meet his level gaze with my own.

"Yes, understood. I have no desire to be kidnapped again. Especially by Gio Conti."

"Good." He unexpectedly delivers a lingering kiss to my lips. It stirs the fires in my pussy, but I know we don't have time.

A tiny moan escapes my lips, betraying my resolve to not give in to his every demand.

"Do I look okay?" I ask as I turn around in a cotton dress that hits just below my knees.

The dress is from one of the designers Dante likes. It's light, sleeveless, black and white striped, and the belt cinches around my waist perfectly. The V-neck shows some cleavage, but not so much as to appear tacky.

Waiting for his response, I fiddle with the engagement ring. It's new and unfamiliar and feels funny on my finger. I don't really have any other jewelry other than the watch he gave me.

Dante casts an appraising eye over me and nods approvingly. "You're beautiful, and stop fussing with the ring; it fits perfectly." He comes over and touches the ring, lifting my hand to his lips and kisses it.

He looks happy, whether for himself or me, or both of us, I don't know. Maybe the ice king is melting after all, though I'm not getting my hopes up that the thaw will come anytime soon.

"I'm sorry. Maybe I'm nervous."

"Juliet, I know you. It takes a lot more than my family to make you nervous." The look in his eyes tells me I'm not as fragile as I make myself out to be.

"Hmm." I find it interesting he says that, considering how unsettling meeting Gio Conti was. The man was a total sleaze. I wouldn't trust him further than I could throw him, and I worry about Dante and his men as they restart their business relationship, knowing how badly it went last time.

"Relax." He drops a light kiss on my painted lips.

"Oh, wait, my purse," I say as I pull away from him and dash into my room to retrieve my designer bag. As soon as I've returned and am within arm's reach, he reaches for my hand and holds it as I walk carefully down the staircase due to the high heels.

"You look so Italian." He chuckles.

"I am Italian."

"I know, but now you dress Italian." His soothing, deep baritone voice caresses my ears, and I melt under his compliment.

Riccardo is waiting for us in the round driveway made of Italian pavers in front of the mansion, and all I need is a formal gown to make me feel like I'm going to a ball. I take it all in—the sound of the birds chirping in the trees that flank the house, the scent of the Tuscan jasmine covering the walls, the sight of the red and white petunias along the walkway by the front door.

Dante helps me into the vehicle, sitting beside me and resting his hand on my thigh. We drive for thirty minutes along winding roads and arrive at a luxurious country house with numerous BMWs, Range Rovers, and a Mercedes.

As we get out, he reiterates that everyone is going to be floored when he shows up with me, as he's never brought a woman to meet his mother before. I take that as a compliment, even though I know the only reason we're doing any of this is to save both our lives.

As we enter the warmly decorated house, it's an open floor plan, more modern than most, with a large family room and a kitchen on the left. There is a huge patio made of pavers at the back, and a row of trees on the right side. It creates a perfect covering for the large table set up for an afternoon feast.

"Dante!" A woman approaches us, in her late fifties judging from the streaks of gray in her hair and the style. She's rapidly removing an apron when her eyes fall on me.

"Mama!" Dante kisses her on both cheeks. "This is Juliet," he continues, and I assume he's saving the big news for later. "Juliet, allow me to introduce my mother, Regina."

"Oh, my dear . . ." She looks me up and down, and for a minute, I think she might cry, then she kisses both my cheeks as I do in return. "Welcome, come in, oh, my hair is a mess. I've been cooking all day, so don't mind me. Come in, come in . . ." She gives Dante a look of approval that she doesn't realize I catch.

She links her arm through mine and escorts me to the patio where the rest of the clan is relaxing over drinks. Dante is so close I can feel his presence even when he's not touching me.

She introduces me first to her son, Sal, who greets me warmly before moving to talk quietly with Dante. Next, I'm introduced to Marcello, the youngest of the three brothers. I assume they all have some hand in the business, and it would be gauche of me to bring it up.

I'm touched by the warm welcome I get. Dante's mother's housekeeper brings out the antipasti as a light summer breeze kicks up. My dress swirls gently around my legs, teasing them with the soft brush of the fabric. It makes me think of Dante's fingers when he's being gentle during sex, but I quickly drag my mind away from any naughty fantasy for now.

His younger brother excuses himself to talk with the guys, and I help his mother in the kitchen and set the table with glasses, then I carry out a pitcher of iced tea and lemonade. His mother keeps trying to shoo me away by saying, "Basta, basta," but I was raised to be helpful, and I'm not used to being waited on by anyone, let alone my future mother-in-law.

"Nessun problema." I fend off her protests and carry out a large plate of veal scallopini with arugula salad on top. She follows behind me with two other side dishes, and I glance over at Dante, who is in a serious conversation with his brothers. Then, I catch Sal slap him on the back in brotherly fashion as they all let out a familiar laugh as if they had a good joke.

I'm wondering what's up. Did they know about Dante's plan? Surely, they are part of the family business. Their dad and grandfather were heads of the entire region in organized crime. They all drive expensive cars, way too expensive for a normal Italian to drive, and they are dressed in nice casual wear with expensive shoes and Rolex watches. Yeah, they've got to be involved.

Then it dawns on me that their mother must know as well, and I realize with a thud that I shouldn't do anything to piss off anyone around this dinner table.

# CHAPTER 23

## DANTE

*I* can tell Juliet and my mother are getting along, and I'm happy and relieved. It buys me time to talk to my brothers on the side and fill them in on the change in direction that Conti has taken, giving in to our demands but then placing the sword of Damocles over our heads at the same time.

My brothers and I decided to increase security so that we don't have a repeat of years ago with hits going out everywhere. It would attract unwanted attention, and the last thing we need is the government breathing down on us day and night and watching our every move. I doubt Conti would like that, with all the skeletons he has in his closet.

We sit down to a family meal with Juliet as the guest of honor. I excuse myself to go into the house and bring out a bottle of Italian sparkling wine, popping it by the table.

"Dante, what are you doing?"

"Well, Mama, it's a special occasion."

"What?" She drags the word out in disbelief that I would have such important news.

I look around the table, making sure I have everyone's attention.

"Juliet and I are getting married. I think that calls for a toast, no?" I look at my mother with slightly raised eyebrows as I continue to fill and hand around the crystal flutes.

After a brief stunned silence, I smile, laugh, raise my own glass to the group, and am the first to lead the toast with a hearty, "Salute." The rest join in, clinking their glasses, and conversation resumes.

The toast might be bittersweet to me but is genuine for everyone else around the table. Even though this is sudden, my brothers help to sell it by adding the traditional 'ha-ha, our brother is no longer a bachelor' guy talk, and they give me a difficult time. But I can tell that deep down they are fine with Juliet and actually hope we'll be happy.

Marchello wanders over and claps me on the shoulder.

"Congratulations, brother. You need companionship however you can get it, and I'm happy for you. I would hate to see you become empty inside like Babbo was before he passed, and I have been worried for years that you've been on the same path."

He's a man of few words, so that's a big speech for him, and I'm touched. When I think about it, Babbo must have been pretty unhappy. When we were younger, I know he had mistresses, but I'm more loyal than that and I don't have any inclination to cheat on Juliet. Should she constantly refuse me in bed, yes, but I don't anticipate that behavior in her. If anything, I think she loves sex as much as I do and looking at her in that elegant but casual dress, I'm struck again by just how beautiful she is. I wouldn't be surprised if she has men checking her out every time she walks down the street, and I'm happy that either Flavio or Enzo will always be with her to make sure she's safe.

Marchello clears his throat quietly and it breaks my reverie.

"So, Conti?"

"I think it's okay. We have associates in the south watching the port and Conti's compound. I'd love to use drones, but of course, they can't be flown at night, and I can't risk Conti's men seeing them."

Marchello looks unconvinced. "So, we're playing a wait and see game of cat and mouse? Conti isn't a patient man."

"No, he's not, so I assume an attack of some kind is forthcoming. If not, then he might hold off indefinitely."

I get up from the table, hinting that the conversation is over. I don't really want to talk business today.

Riccardo takes his food break, eating in the kitchen, then patrols the grounds until we all leave together after the sun has set. There's a happening nightlife here, same as in most large cities, so my brothers decide we need a night on the town with Juliet to show her a good time.

We find parking and walk along the Arno. The heat of the day is dissipating, and I wrap my arm around Juliet to make sure she doesn't stumble on the uneven cobblestones. The drivers are crazy at all times of the day and night, so my eyes are peeled for any trouble. Riccardo keeps watch too.

On a whim, we stop at an outdoor café, order a bottle of red wine, and each have a glass. We sit and talk as poor Juliet gets peppered with questions from my brothers, who have taken a shine to her. She takes it all in good humor, and I relax—it's going well, and they like her. That's one item I can take off my worry list.

I sit back and enjoy the night as the little lights hang from the outdoor awnings. Occasionally, people walk by, and I catch fragments of their conversations floating on the wind, conversations about boys, girls, office gossip. I don't have that type of life, never have, and spending time with Juliet is showing me that I'm missing something.

I casually glance over to my fiancée, who is so animated as she speaks intensely about her favorite Italian painter. Her passion for art comes out as my brothers sit enthralled.

She's vibrant and she brings out the best in me, the part I'd buried long ago. I sip my wine as I take in the three of them and commit this picture to my memory. It's beautiful, a surprise I didn't know I was eager for. But now it's happened, I understand my brothers going through strife when a woman they fall for doesn't feel the same.

How does Juliet feel about me, anyway? We haven't talked about that. She doesn't cower from me, which is a good start, and I'm dead sure she'd be happy for me to take her home tonight and fuck her royally. She feels my eyes on her and gracefully turns her head in my direction. Her tiny smile is more beautiful than any lipstick or gloss she could use, and it shines brighter than the most brilliant diamond.

She lifts her glass to her lips that I long to taste again. I imagine licking the thick red Chianti from them, kissing her as I trickle wine from my mouth into hers. My cock is excited and I'm antsy for an excuse to rub it against her, so I decide it's time we hit the clubs.

I pay the bill, generously tipping our server.

"The clubs should be hopping now. Let's try the one downtown, you know, our favorite," Marchello suggests.

"Good idea, let's walk."

Instantly, Riccardo is on the move, blending in with the shadows on the street without a word.

Fifteen minutes later, we are at a club called Jab. I hear techno music and sirens from inside and give my brothers a skeptical look. "Are we really doing this?"

"Please. It will be fun. I haven't been to many clubs, and I've been cooped up for so long," Juliet begs me.

Any reservations I had melt away when I catch the imploring look in her eyes. We enter Jab, with its techno lights and pounding music. I'm dreading this as it's a younger crowd, but having Juliet on my arm helps a lot. She looks hot even though she's not in a party dress, and she pulls me to the dance floor. It's some song she likes about Paris, and although I've never heard it before, it's mainstream enough that I can handle it. I take her hand and pull her into my chest, and when she moves her body against mine, I almost explode in my slacks.

I look down into her dark eyes, almost onyx in the low light, and gaze at her jet-black hair and olive skin. I realize she's everything I've ever wanted in a woman and more. She's survived kidnapping, meeting her father who is a notorious psychopath, and now, my family.

We get lost in the music as she wraps her arms around my neck and my lips find hers. The entire club and music fade as I get lost in her. She's everything I'm not—good, sweet, pure, honest. I need her. I want her. I just need to figure out how to neutralize Conti as we can't live with him in our world. It's too dangerous.

The song comes to an end, and as we break away, Riccardo is walking around the club talking to other men on our payroll. My capo, Lucca Donatello, is here, and if he's here, it can't be good.

I pull Juliet off the floor. She wants to stay and party, but it might not be safe.

"Juliet, we have to go."

"But we just got here."

"For once, just do as I say. We need to go."

I motion to my brothers, who are dancing with some girls, and we make a quick exit to our team standing by the door.

"We have picked up intel that Conti wants to kill you in a way that looks like an accident," my capo informs me with a solemn face. "Sorry, wish I had better news. You're not safe anywhere."

"Fuck," I explode, punching the wall behind me.

"We need to move, now," Riccardo stresses the urgency, and my brothers lead the way out with other members of our organization who will stay with them until this is over.

"All right." I turn to Juliet, who's in shock and shaking.

Sal takes off his jacket and puts it over her shoulders before heading to his car. We slide into the car that's waiting for us out front. As we drive off, I notice that Juliet is quiet, which isn't like her.

"It will be okay."

"No, it won't. I'm young, I don't want to die."

"I'll do everything in my power to fix this."

"I thought you said he would back off now that we've announced our engagement. What happened to that being the fix? Why isn't that enough for him?"

"I don't know. But he's relentless. And he has no regard for human life, less than most men in our business," I whisper.

She doesn't answer me, just stares out the window.

Our driver speeds out of the city, and Riccardo suggests that we stay on the move, which I agree with. So, when we get home, we need to pack and take the jet somewhere and keep moving until Conti is neutralized... in an acceptable fashion. Whacking another don will only start another bloodbath. I'm already forming a plan of where to go, and we'll use a different jet in order to cover our tracks as much as possible.

Juliet stops my train of thought. "We have the university event tomorrow," she reminds me.

"Fuck me, so we do," I groan, stroking a finger along my chin. "Well, we'll go, get in and get out quickly, then take off from there."

Riccardo doesn't look happy about that. "You sure, boss?"

"I think it will be fine. The press will be there, and that would be too public for him to bring that kind of heat on himself." I'm trying to convince myself as much as convince him.

"Okay, boss, I'll have men everywhere."

"But keep it discreet. We don't want to let Conti know we're on to him."

He nods in comprehension. "Capisco."

We arrive at the house and wait in the car until Riccardo and Lucca clear it, then they come out and open our doors.

"We're good, for now."

I take Juliet's hands in mine and address her seriously before we get out of the car. Tears are forming in her eyes. "We need to be careful. I assumed your father would be happy to find you after all these years, but apparently, he has decided you're a liability. But don't worry," I lean over and wipe a tear away with my thumb, "it will be okay. I'll figure it out."

# CHAPTER 24

JULIET

$\mathcal{W}$e return to the mansion very late. I hate Dante for pulling me into this world, but even though it's hard to admit it, I love him. As dark and brooding and messed up as he is, I like it when he gives me the look that tells me he wants me, now, on my knees or bent over a table.

I slide off the jacket Sal loaned me. His family is sweet, not at all the monsters I was expecting.

Dante takes the jacket from me. "Go up, it's late," he says softly, cupping my face and chin with his right hand, making me look at him. "I'll make this right. Please don't hate me. I can't bear it if you hate me."

I nod as another tear escapes my eye. He wipes it away and kisses my lips tenderly.

"I'll be up in a minute."

I walk slowly up the staircase and realize how tired I am. The stairs might as well be a mountain.

Dante talks to his capo, a tall man in his late twenties who I've never been able to figure out. His face never changes, and he never pays any attention to me or anyone else in the room except to know what our position is and to determine if we're a friend or foe in a split second. He's calm under pressure, unwavering, and never distracted.

I make my way to a window on the top floor that overlooks the large driveway with dozens of black vehicles pulling up. There must be a meeting.

I don't know what to do in this situation. Dante may be up all night with the men, but he said he'd be up. Do I go to bed or sit vigil? There's no how-to manual on what's appropriate under the circumstances and it's not exactly something you can look up on Google.

I take a quick shower in case something happens and nervously towel off while keeping an ear out. I have a towel around me when Dante walks in.

"How are you, babe?"

"Umm," I grumble as I'm not sure.

He wraps his arms around me. "Go to bed. I'll be up as soon as I can."

"All right."

I throw on an old pair of boy shorts and a black tank top, then crawl onto the humongous bed. It's so empty without him. I need Dante beside me, because good or bad, he's our best shot at surviving this, and I pray his brothers are safe given what's transpired in the past. I hope Conti isn't planning to repeat history, but I know better than to think otherwise now. It scares me to think that I've become so knowledgeable in such a short time.

I'm drifting in and out of sleep when I suddenly wake to the sound of shouting and crashing glass. It's very close. I open my eyes and a man dressed in black is in our room, attacking Dante with a knife as Dante reaches for his gun.

I scramble out of bed, adrenaline racing, and hide behind the mattress with my knees on the tiled floor as I watch the men wrestle.

I hear a clatter and realize the intruder has knocked the gun from Dante's hand. Quickly, I scuttle over to retrieve it and aim, firing at the intruder without thinking twice. He's in my home and hurting my man, and all the hatred toward a father who turned my life into this is in that one squeeze of the trigger. The man drops, no longer a threat. Dante feels for a pulse, then he looks at me.

"He's dead."

I can't believe I took a life. I'm not proud of it, but it was a question of survival. My instincts took over and it was as if I wasn't even in my body, it was like it was some other person who took that man's last breath from him.

I'm still kneeling from where I took my shot when the room starts filling with Dante's men.

I hear sirens, and I wonder if I'll be arrested. I can't stop shaking even though Dante's warm arms are wrapped around me.

I almost slip into unconsciousness until a man runs smelling salts under my nose. When I come to, Dante is holding my hand, and Commissioner Manara has arrived; the body has been removed from the room, and I remember what transpired.

"There are warrants out for Conti's arrest for extortion at the port and the murder of two judges in the case against his top-ranking consigliere. So, he's like a trapped animal with nothing left to lose," Commissioner Manara says to Dante.

"Hmm, that makes him even more dangerous than usual," I comment.

"Exactly." Dante kisses my head to reassure me, and I snuggle into him, trying to forget the sight of the blood-stained tile in our bedroom.

"Miss Accordi, are you sure you didn't know the deceased? We've associated him with a known organized crime boss."

"I never saw him before tonight."

"Do you want me to call anyone for you?" The detective has seen much in what I estimate must be his twenty years of experience. He's a handsome man with curly, thick, dark brown hair and eyes. He has a notebook in his hand and jots down a few things quickly.

He already checked out our driver's licenses and probably ran our background checks. I wonder if he knows who my intended husband is behind the façade of Micheli Enterprises.

"No, I'd rather my parents not hear that way. We just got engaged, and we haven't had time to visit them to tell them."

He nods in understanding. "That visit might have to be postponed. I can put you in police protection, but your fiancé has declined the offer."

"I'm fine. I trust my fiancé."

"Have you ever met Conti?"

"Not that I know of," I fib. I'm not sure how much they know if Conti has been under surveillance, but I'm certain they didn't have men inside the Duomo.

"Do you have somewhere to go that's safe, unknown to anyone?"

"Yes, I do." Dante is quietly confident.

And that's it. Someone packs a bag for us and we're on the move. Dante is adamant that he's more capable of keeping us safe than the police, but he takes the Commissioner's business card just the same.

We're cautioned not to leave the country and Dante carries me to the Rover as Riccardo slips behind the wheel of the car. As we pull away, the lights of every emergency vehicle except a fire truck are visible.

Dante is still talking about my great shot, amazed.

"Where did you learn to shoot? It's not possible to shoot like that your first time."

"Hunting with Dad every Christmas."

He throws back his head and laughs out loud, and I smile. I can still surprise him. I take a second to relish this before I rest my head on his shoulder as we head to the airport. I don't know where we're going, and I don't care. All I know is we can't stay in our home and being on the run is the safest for now.

We arrive at the airport and walk through the darkness, and

although I'm too tired to look at my watch, the air is cool and damp and it seems close to dawn.

We board the plane without a word and take off as the sun comes over the horizon. I wonder how long we'll be on the run, and what awaits us at our next destination.

"Where are we going?"

"Capri. It will be packed with tourists and there are places where we can hide out. I have houses no one knows about all over Italy."

Of course, he does. I notice then that he's favoring his right arm.

"What happened?"

"Just a little sore from the knife cutting me. It's nothing to worry about, gorgeous. They stitched me up and I had a whiskey for the pain." He grins, but I'm not convinced.

"Well, I want to check it later."

"Okay, I'll let you, but only if you promise to stop worrying."

I can't believe he's almost teasing me at a time like this. "I can't do that," I say as I shake my head. "A psycho is chasing us."

"We'll find him. My men are good."

I wonder if they are good enough.

I put my hand on his thigh and look at my engagement ring. I wonder if it's worth it. Why not just change my name and move? But it's a short-term solution to a long-term problem—we'll never be free until that man is dead.

I'm sure the Commissioner knows more than he was saying, but as long as we are free and it was a justified shooting, I think we're in the clear.

I fall asleep on my sexy fiancé and wake just before landing. As I take in the majestic view of the azure water below us, I think a change of scenery is just what I need.

# CHAPTER 25

## JULIIET

The hotel we arrive at is just as grand as the one in Milan, but I doubt it's one he owns as that would be too obvious. I don't know the details and I'm fine with that as long as I always have a guard or Dante with me.

The balcony doors are open, and the sheer curtains billow gently in the sea breeze as if they haven't a care in the world. For a moment, I mourn the simple life that is now lost to me.

What's the phrase, be careful what you wish for?

I had no way of knowing what a more exciting life would mean. I would have been happy just going out to clubs and having a boyfriend. Finishing school, starting a career, and going home to visit my parents without it requiring an entourage of expensive vehicles that would raise more than a few eyebrows in our sleepy town.

I look at my lover pacing on the balcony. The five o'clock shadow on his jaw has filled in, giving him even more sex appeal. I want him... God help me, I can't keep my hands off him, and when he touches me, I forget everything around me.

I don't want anyone else. Good or bad, he's loyal. Do I have deep-seated daddy issues stemming from the adoption? Maybe.

Would I act differently if this wasn't how my life unfolded? I'm not so sure. What is fate and what is up to pure chance? I don't know. I'm just glad we're all alive. Dante has been in contact with his brothers, who are hiding out for a few days, so that's a relief.

I shiver even though it's a perfectly sunny Italian day.

"Can I get you anything?" Dante stands in the doorway and the look of tenderness in his eyes speaks volumes.

"You," I reply as I lean back against the pillows on the bed.

"Me?" he teases.

Some people say the thrill of being next to death makes people horny. I don't need an excuse. As he approaches, I'm all his as he takes his dress shirt off and lets it fall softly to the carpet, followed by his belt and loafers.

We take advantage of the quiet, empty room and are deliberate as we help each other out of our clothing. I breathe him in, and it's Italian leather mixed with salty air. It fills my nostrils as I close my eyes and run my hands through his thick hair. He drops kisses on my neck, and there's a change in him.

Up until now, he's always been rough with me, but today, he takes his time. I'm the only thing on his mind as his lips tenderly descend on mine and I raise my head to meet him halfway.

I run my hands over his back and bring them to his chest, raking my fingers through his chest hair and grabbing his nipples. I tug and pinch them until he winces, and he gives me a grin that changes from shock at first to pleasure.

I lick one nipple and then the other, circling them with my damp tongue until they harden. I run my hand down his arm to the bandage where the knife cut him, then I lift it to my lips and kiss it.

The salty air fills the room as tiny beads of perspiration break out across my back and he takes my breast into his mouth. A moan escapes into the breeze as my back arches. He glides his fingers into me as if to ready my pussy for his throbbing cock, but there's no need.

The dampness between my legs is more than enough for him to

enter me. Leaning to one side, he plunges into me, and I twist and moan under him, then I hear him gasp as I take all of him as he thrusts deeper and deeper.

Lifting my hips to move with him, I'm no longer a victim but a partner, and he rolls us over so that I'm on top of him. I lean down to lick his neck and my long, straight hair cascades over him like a waterfall, his head sinking deeper into the pillow as I grind my hips over his. I tilt my head back and my mind soars in an ecstasy that is indescribable.

I look down at him as he puts his hands on my hips, moving them back and forth on his hard cock. He's a perfect lover, knowing just how and where to touch and stroke me to bring about the ultimate pleasure as he hits all the right spots inside me.

The pressure tells me that my orgasm is approaching, but I want him to come with me. I open my eyes and he meets my gaze as we cry out together. Wave after wave of pleasure surges through our bodies, and as he calls out my name, my pussy quivers around him. Afterward, I slump into his chiseled chest while he's still hard inside me, but he's short of breath, so I move off him, and a rush of air pushes between us until I snuggle up to him and he wraps his arm around me.

He pulls me closer, my hair tangled between us and damp around my face, beads of perspiration dripping between my breasts.

"You're amazing," he whispers. "I love you."

Did he really just say he loves me? Wow. I enjoy the sheer joy of this for a second before I respond.

"I love you, too."

The moment is interrupted by an alert on his phone that Riccardo is at the door with brunch.

I pull on lightweight tracksuit pants and a black T-shirt, and Dante finds a pair of jeans and a polo shirt in his luggage. God, he's handsome in everything. He makes the clothes look good, and everything he does is a confident move, never flustered, but for a moment, his mind clearly has flashed back to the attack.

"You know, I should have had that guy at the house. I said I'd protect you." His eyes are filled with sadness and disappointment in himself.

"We got this. It all worked out." I shrug. "Can I open the door?"

"No, I will," he says, and he moves ahead of me, looks through the peephole in the thick door, and texts Riccardo. Only when he hears back does he open the door.

Riccardo rolls in a cart with hot food and cold juice and motions for Dante to join him on the balcony, where he pulls out his vape pen and sucks on it profusely.

I take this as a sign that there must be something bad going on with our situation, but at this moment, I don't care. Instead, I take the opportunity to shove down some hot eggs and coffee. O-M-G, coffee! I was getting a headache, but this will surely cure it. I can't remember the last time I had caffeine... probably yesterday afternoon before we left his mother's house.

The bed is torn apart from our lovemaking, so after getting my coffee, I pull a chair from the desk to sit on. The guys return and Dante snacks on some Danish—I don't know how he stays so slim. He gulps coffee and asks if I'm okay, assuring me that he'll get me anything I want.

I smile. "I'm fine, really." The truth is, between the commotion of last night, the flight, the sea air, and the most incredible fucking sex of my life, I'm drained. I'm happy just to sit and admire him standing across from me, knowing that he loves me and that I'm wearing his ring. I can't wait until we are free from this intricate web of survival and are able to simply enjoy that.

"We have men around and we're trying to locate Conti. I have a plan, but it's dangerous. Do you want out? I can try to change your name. I can get you out of the country. That might be the safest thing to do."

"No, I'm safer with you," I insist, and our eyes meet over our coffee cups as we commit to seeing this through to the bitter end. "I won't rest until that man is gone. I'm not safe anywhere. He has as many resources as you, maybe more."

He nods. "Okay then," he raises his coffee cup, "to the end of all this."

I raise my cup to him, and we sip.

"What now?" I ask.

"We're going to Milan, to our penthouse."

Did he just say 'our'? Fuck me.

"But he knows it's yours. It's your hotel."

"Exactly," he says, and he flashes me a smile like a cat who swallowed the cream.

We finish our coffee and take a shower together, running soap over each other's toned bodies, enjoying the confinement of the shower stall, and drying each other off before we get dressed to hit the road again.

I take one last look out the balcony doors and make a note to come back here for a vacation, just the two of us. Riccardo and Flavio can take a hike for a day.

We follow our detail to the SUV and make our journey back to the airport. Now that we've regrouped, I try to act more confident —that we'll be okay. Dante seems sure of himself, and the men around us move with such practiced moves. I know he's got the best men on our protection detail.

Yet in my gut, I have a feeling it's only a matter of time until I meet the man who gave me life again. And I'm not looking forward to it.

# CHAPTER 26

JULIET

*B*ack on the tarmac in Milan, I walk a step behind Dante as we approach the SUV. Not because I am subservient, but out of respect and for safety. Riccardo wants guards around me as, apparently, I'm the fatted calf that Conti wants served on a gold platter.

Is it easy to be abducted? Sure, especially if you know that person. Is it easy to fall in love with a seductive Italian with an unlimited credit card and a flair for fun, food, designer everything, and an insatiable appetite for sex? You bet.

Alone in the back of the vehicle, Dante looks at me seriously. "I have a plan," he whispers, taking my hand and wrapping both of his around it as he looks me in the eye. "But first, tell me this. If we come through this, will you marry me, Juliet?"

My stomach does a somersault like the Olympic gold medal hinges on my gymnastics performance. My breath catches in my throat, and I choke back saliva.

He asked me to marry him, and it's not just for show or to keep me safe. He wants me.

"Yes," flies out of my mouth. Because I'm addicted to him, his smell, his sometimes rough demeanor, his dreamy eyes that can turn cold on a dime, and his hands that can caress or slap my ass. And I'm definitely addicted to sex with him.

"Yes?" He chuckles.

"Yes," I reply, and I make a feeble attempt to slap his chest for prying me for more in my answer.

"Then it's settled."

And I close my eyes as his lips cover mine, gentle at first, then rougher, more demanding and I like it. I love this man that loves to be in control, and I love him taking control in the bedroom too. With him, I feel safe.

I smile and bat my eyes at him, not on purpose but because we're bantering, and I like this new version of us. No more do I have to give him shit just to get my way with him.

I'm dressed casually, and so is Dante, in an attempt to blend in. His enemies will be looking for him in his designer suits and not in jeans and a t-shirt like we both came out of a pit at a grunge band concert.

We drive toward the city center and I'm looking forward to knowing my way around this time. I mean, not the streets and all, but the hotel and the penthouse. We had a good time here.

We take the familiar elevator, but unfortunately, we can't fool around anywhere as Dante's all business, and I should be too. But the man just asked me to marry him for real and I can't wait to make love to him again, without the crisis hanging over our heads. For all I know, this could go on for weeks or more.

We're whisked into our penthouse, and I'm surprised to see that our guards are different. I ask Dante about it, but he says everyone is where they are supposed to be.

I'm putting my life in his hands again, and I wonder if that's a smart move. I don't like not knowing what is going to happen next, but I know our security team has to be fluid and make adjustments as needed to keep us as safe as they can until the threat is over.

"So how much is the hit on my head?" I try to be flippant, but I'm stressed as I pace the penthouse.

"Enough," Riccardo says, and I'm surprised. It's not that he can't talk to me, he just normally chooses not to. I think killing an intruder made my stock go up with him.

"Hmm." I go to the kitchen and warm up the espresso machine. I don't want to distract the men from their planning and from the hotel blueprints spread out over the table. I make espresso for everyone, and as I set the cup in front of my fiancé, I gently brush my fingers over his forearm. I get goosebumps and I notice the hair on his arm stands up as well. I smile to myself, knowing he's experiencing the connection too. He loves me.

I don't know what to do with myself. I'm not part of the plan they are cooking up, so I turn on the TV more for background noise than anything. I text my mom and Ava that I'll see them soon.

Apparently, Ava is still carrying on with her Italian hottie. Of course, she has no idea who mine is, but I told her I found someone.

Knowing how Conti is, I wonder again what happened to my mother. Dante said he found a friend of hers who told him that she must have left Italy... or Conti did something to her. I may never know.

"Can I do anything?" I ask Dante and Riccardo. They are deep in their discussion. I assume I'm interrupting them, but I want to.

"No, babe, we're fine. Maybe bring us some scotch and figure out a late lunch?"

"Sure. You want me to call food up? Are we using room service?"

"Oh, right, no, we don't want anyone to know that we're really here. Better to send Flavio, anything you want."

"Okay."

I bring over three rocks glasses of scotch, neat, and set them on the dining room table. Then I look up restaurants on my phone to see what kind of sandwiches we can get. I put together a list on my phone so I can text it, and my stomach starts to rumble.

"Yeah, it's inevitable, the only question is what time he'll be here." It's a statement, not a question as Riccardo takes a sip of his drink.

"Our sources say he's en route, so that should be about sundown. We need to get food and then lay low. We have lookouts at the inbound roads and the perimeter of the hotel," Dante adds.

Flavio nods. "Good, gotcha. I got our best men on it, just like you wanted, boss."

"Thanks." Dante claps him on the back, something I've never seen him do before.

I text Flavio the food order without bothering to order wine as well. I've already checked the fully stocked built-in wine cabinet and figure we're good to go there. Of course, I can't get tipsy; I still need to be able to function.

"Do I have a part in all this?"

"I got it covered." Dante picks up his drink and drains the liquor in his glass. I consider it to be similar to drinking kerosene, but he seems to like it. All the men do.

He sets his glass down. "I think we're ready."

"Ready as we'll ever be," Riccardo reiterates as he drinks more scotch before rolling up the blueprints.

Flavio heads out to get the food, returning half an hour later. We sit in uneasy silence, like we're at a party together but nobody knows each other.

I get an uneasy feeling and I wonder if everyone will make it through the night. It's apparent that something huge is going down, but I have no idea what.

Maybe it's better I don't know.

# CHAPTER 27

## DANTE

The evening is setting in, but there's still a glow of light on the horizon. If Conti doesn't arrive soon, we'll have to deal with him and his entourage in the dark, and I don't want that.

Conti takes entitlement to the next level. I never want to be that way, and I'm glad Juliet didn't inherit those traits from him. I'm happy her mom sacrificed everything to keep her safe—yet here I come, barreling in to right an old wrong. I may mess it all up for both of them, though I hope not.

"Thanks for the food, babe." I give Juliet a small smile that comes up more on one side than the other to create a wink. It's my typical lady-killer look for when I really want to get lucky. I'm going to need all my luck tonight.

Even with all the drama going on, we've kept our wits about us, and I hope things are resolved tonight and I'm able to protect everyone.

My brothers are in safe houses as I guessed Conti would make multiple strikes. When Riccardo hears through his mic that Conti's getting closer, I walk to my room and suit up in tactical wear, returning with a thin vest.

"Hey, babe," I say as I pull Juliet into my broad chest, "I want you to wear this." She slips her arms into the garment. "Just wear it, no questions, please." I give her another jacket to put over it that's light and looks like a workout jogger jacket.

"Dante, what is all this? What are you doing?"

"Keeping you safe."

Riccardo and Flavio get another update, and it's time to play our game.

"Come on, babe. We're going to the rooftop."

"What rooftop?"

"You'll see," I say with a smile as I pick up a bag of gear and we head up just as night falls.

I know she's curious as to what's in the bag. It's my end-of-the-world bag.

We all enter the elevator and get off on the roof, one floor above the rooms. It's gorgeous up here, with a huge pool, a restaurant, and outside tables. I love this place. The ambiance at night is perfectly romantic as it overlooks the most beautiful part of Milan.

"This is amazing," Juliet says. "But isn't this unsafe?" she asks. I'm sure her mind is racing through scenarios. We don't have much cover, and it's dark.

"One might think so," I reply with a devilish grin as I hoist my bag further up my shoulder.

Just as night falls, I hear the fire alarm go off in the hotel.

I nod to Riccardo and Flavio as we fist-bump each other and chuckle nervously.

"Do or die," we say in unison as everyone on the rooftop gets up to evacuate, leaving their dinners and drinks behind. I'm thinking this is going to be an expensive night, losing the revenue from all this food, but fuck it. I peer over the edge of the roof onto the street. It looks like the hotel has about emptied with minimum chaos, but hopefully enough to throw off or slow down Commissioner Manara.

"You know, Gio Conti is going to be like a fish swimming upstream," I snicker.

"Yeah, poor fuck." Flavio grins.

I put Juliet behind the bar and make her promise she will not get up, no matter what, and shove a 9mm in her hand.

Only the pool shows any semblance of normalcy. The ambient lights at the outdoor restaurant and bar are further in the distance, and the rest of the rooftop is empty.

The guys and I have all taken cover when the elevator doors ding open.

"Come out, you fucking scumbag," Conti rasps. Juliet must be scared to death, but we agreed she was safest with us. I hope she covers her ears soon as I forgot to warn her.

"Fuck off, old man," I taunt him.

Conti's men shoot off a few rounds of rapid-fire machine guns, and I'm wondering how we will compete with that, though we're not totally naked out here.

"Yeah, if you want your daughter back, keep walking," I call out again.

Conti and his men duck behind trash cans for cover, then there is a flash bang, and my ears ring. Gunfire is exchanged again as we shoot in all directions like in an old-fashioned Western.

I hear a squeal, and my heart is in my throat. Someone has picked up Juliet and is carting her around like a cat by the scruff of her neck. She tries to fend off her foe to no avail as he must have caught her off guard and taken the 9mm from her. The man exclaims, "Got her."

He drags her to Conti, who is still alive and not among the few dead men on the ground.

"Ahh," he drawls, pulling Juliet in front of the pool. The lighted water never looked so inviting and yet so deadly at the same time. "Dante, you son of a bitch, show your face. I got your woman."

I come out to face Juliet, and I pray Riccardo is in place. He was a crack sniper back in the day.

"You're such a cowardly scumbag," I sneer at Conti over the pool. "You take women and children and sell them into sex dungeons, and now, you're willing to kill your daughter."

"Shut up, Dante. I can and will do whatever I like. That's what made me the richest and most powerful don in all of Italy." He grabs Juliet by the hair and, with a knife to her throat, holds her in front of him as a human shield.

Juliet is clearly shocked, but I can see her survival instincts are taking over as she looks to me for direction. Her eyes meet mine.

And that's when I wink at her. She takes it as a moment of opportunity, using her elbow to jab Conti as hard as possible in the ribs, and makes to get away. A single bullet flies through the air unseen and Conti drops, but not before three more shots are fired that kill off the last of his men.

Juliet is on all fours on the ground, and after a quick look to make sure my men are all right, I run to her and pick her up, frantically checking her over to make sure she's not been nicked.

"I'm fine. Is he dead?"

"Yes."

"Good. Can we get out of here?"

"I'm sure there will be tons of questions when the cops get here."

"Yeah, about that . . ." For a moment, I'm quiet. "I taped the entire ordeal for Manara, and we used ourselves to lure him here. They wanted me to get Conti to confess to his crimes, but when you were held hostage, there wasn't time. We'll destroy our guns and not talk to the police or anyone else. We don't know who shot him. Remember, Juliet, it's all a blur, and you were in shock."

"You didn't tell Manara about the fire alarm either." It dawns on her as a sly smile breaks out on her face.

"That might have slipped my mind," I confess, and we both have a good chuckle.

Riccardo races around collecting our weapons and takes the service elevator down to the street to dispose of the incriminating evidence.

"So, who takes over for Conti now? That's how it works, right?"

"Yes, probably his underboss or a son. God, I hope he's someone who has a better moral compass," I groan.

It's like any work situation where your coworkers don't play nice in the sandbox. Only in my world—it can be deadly.

## CHAPTER 28

### JULIET

*W*hen I started college, I didn't know who I was. I felt like an oddball and a bit of a nerd even though I attended a prestigious art college. I would have never guessed in my wildest dreams that I came from a notorious crime family that was shrouded in death and suffering at the hands of my father.

And if you told me I would fall in love with my kidnapper, and that he'd save me from my ruthless father, who would rather have me dead than make a business deal with his rival, well, I wouldn't have believed you.

But here we are, at my parents' house in Greve, the sleepy little town that harvests olives and grapes. It's the beginning of grape-picking season and the streets are busier than usual. There will be some small events going on for the locals to celebrate, and many will drink too much wine.

Dante is sitting in less formal attire, but he's still smoking hot, so much so that I have a mind to take him to the cellar and let him fuck me against the wall like he did in his kitchen. God knows I want to, but when I scream, "Fuck me harder," I'm sure my parents would hear, and there's no coming back from that.

His face is tanned from our short getaway to Capri to erase

some of the bad memories. I still have nightmares some nights, either about the life I took, even though he was an intruder who would have killed me, or about being held by Conti on the night he was killed, afraid he'd slit my throat and throw me in the swimming pool.

Dante tells me this is all normal and will go away in time, some old adage about time healing all wounds. We never could trace my birth mother or her family anywhere, so if she got away from him alive, I hope she knows her sacrifices weren't in vain and that I'm happy.

"So, what kind of music do you listen to?" Dad asks my fiancé as they wander off to another room to have some guy talk. To my parents, Dante is just a successful businessman, and if they suspect more, they are too polite to mention it.

Ava has joined us on the trip to Greve and is full of energy, getting me caught up on the last two weeks. She's in love with my engagement ring and has declared Dante a catch. She's supposed to fly back to New York when her class is over, but she's toying with the idea of staying longer as she adores the Italian way of life. She still has the boy toy—he has a real name, and I really should use it, but I just can't get over the fact that he looks like he's sixteen.

We have plenty of wine on the table, and Ava and I help Mama set the table and fold the linen napkins before bringing out the food. My parents' wine is nowhere near the price point of Dante's collection, but he's not complaining, and I think he's actually enjoying the company and conversation today.

As he whispered to me right before we arrived at the house, he's never had to meet a lover's mother before, let alone his new fiancées, so he was concerned that she might not be impressed by him.

I said, "Dante, you have a degree from a prestigious college, you run a multi-million-euro business, and you're committed to giving back to the community. Don't worry about it. All any mother wants is for her children to be happy."

He thinks for a second. "You're right." With a new bounce in his step, he casually walked up to my mother, greeted her with a kiss on each cheek, and gave her the flowers we'd brought with a flourish. And that was it, she loved him right away.

I had to tell Ava not to spill the beans to my parents about the lie to the dean that I was with my sick grandmother, when in fact, I was with Dante. She swore she would lock that in the vault forever.

I hope Conti's children never come to power. I'm happy if we never hear the name again. I couldn't tell Ava the truth, I mean, I wouldn't believe it if someone told me everything I've been through in the past month and threw in an adoption cover-up on top of everything else. I'd call your bluff for sure.

So, our secrets are all safe, and we live to fight another day.

Something else that came out of this was that I realized I loved Dante so much, I wanted to work with him in some capacity. So, I went to work for a top-of-the-line interior design company in Florence and I'm learning how to refurbish Dante's hotels and restaurants when they need it. I still draw on the side, and Dante is going to hang some of my work around the house when I finish it.

We've been working so much that it's hard to find time for special extracurricular activities that occur outside of the bedroom if you get my drift. But my man loves to color outside the box, and I'm more than okay with that. I like keeping things new and interesting.

My mother is buzzing around with wedding talk. It's too hot to have a summer wedding these days, so we're thinking in the fall or next spring. I don't care one way or the other, but my mother is overjoyed, and no doubt she'll be wanting grandkids soon. But for now, Dante and I are content getting to know each other and learning how to live and work together while not smothering each other. I know, a bad reference for a person in organized crime, but it is what it is.

We have the rest of our lives to figure each other out, have loud arguments, and even louder make-up sex. My future husband has my number there, and I have to admit, I've become a bit of a dirty girl. I love him and love making love to him—day, night, you name it. It will be one exciting ride being in this crazy family, and now that we know Conti is gone, we're free to travel and explore anywhere we want without looking over our shoulders. That sure sounds like freedom to me!

But we all know there is a price to pay for freedom. One never knows what is lurking around the corner. Particularly for the Micheli family.

Want more Dante and Juliet? I've written a special bonus chapter for them! It's exclusively for my readers! Sign up and get it now!
Dante & Juliet's Bonus Scene
Or use this link in your browser
https://geni.us/IKingBonusScene

Do you want to read more about The Micheli Family? Book #2 continues with Dante's brother Sal and the twisted fate that brings another Conti into their midst. Only this time, she's Gio's gorgeous daughter who is out for revenge.

Continue reading Dirty Vengeance: A Dark Mafia Romance (Micheli Mafia) Book 2 where passion burns between Sal and the woman who stalks him. This book is full of unexpected twists and turns and sets up book #3.

In Dirty Vengeance, Gio Conti's daughter, Francesca, is after revenge, and suspicion rests on the Michelis. She is on a quest to find who killed her father, but more importantly, she needs to find her best friend, Sophia. She was being abused by her husband and wound up missing. And we all know what happens to unwanted mafia wives in southern Italy. . . they live in a compound with the others, or worse, sold into human trafficking.

Francesca has no love loss for her psycho brothers who want to cut her out of the family business. But they'd better think twice after they play her for a fool as she seeks revenge on Sal Micheli at the half-masked ball of the year in Florence. This is where the families gather and conduct business under the noses of the powers who govern. Elite socialites feed the underground with their need for illegal drugs and gambling addictions.

If you liked Italian King, continue reading Dirty Vengeance, book 2 in the series!

# PREQUEL TO THE VOLKOV BRATVA

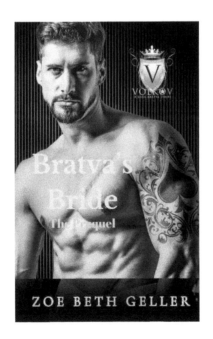

Bratva's Bride
At my shop!

# ALSO BY ZOE BETH GELLER

Stop by **shopzoebethgeller.com** and get your pre-orders early. I offer bundle deals, audio, books in German, and so much more! Get releases first on in my shop!

**Dirty: A Dark Mafia Romance Series**

**Micheli Mafia**

Italian King: A Dark Mafia Romance Book 1

Dirty Vengeance: A Dark Mafia Romance Book 2

Dirty Bargain: A Dark Mafia Romance Book 3

Dirty Born: A Dark Mafia Romance Book 4

Dirty Deals: A Dark Mafia Romance Book 5

**Volkov Bratva**

King's Promise

Brutal Promise

Sinful Promise

**Borrelli Mafia**

Mafia King: Matteo

Zoe's Facebook fan group

ZBG Mafia Romance

**Maine Megaladons Football Series**

Faking it with the Football Star

The Player's Obsession

Scoring with the Coach's Daughter

**Maine Maulers Hockey Series**

Maine Maulers Hockey Series

Rookie in Love (now in audio)

Jagged Ice

Hotter than Puck

Benched by the Nanny

Puck in the Oven

Pucking the Team Captain

Pucking with the Goalie

**Sin Bin Hockey Series**

Tyler: Hooked (Free prequel to the series)

The Sin Bin Hockey Series

Jackson: Against the Boards

Alan: Between the Pipes

Erik: Fire and Ice

Blayze: Slap Shot

Paavo: The Defender

Spencer: Penalty Box

Isak: Coach

Kaden: Game Time

Liam: The Enforcer

Jake: Roughing

Facebook fan group for sports

Zoe Beth Geller's Hockey Pond Reader